Also by Kathleen Hale

No One Else Can Have You

NOTHING BAD IS GOING TO HAPPEN

Kathleen Hale

HARPER TEEN
An Imprint of HarperCollinsPublishers

HarperTeen is an imprint of HarperCollins Publishers.

Nothing Bad Is Going to Happen
Copyright © 2016 by Full Fathom Five, LLC
All rights reserved. Printed in the United States of America.
No part of this book may be used or reproduced in any manner
whatsoever without written permission except in the case of brief
quotations embodied in critical articles and reviews. For information
address HarperCollins Children's Books, a division of HarperCollins
Publishers, 195 Broadway, New York, NY 10007.
www.epicreads.com

Library of Congress Cataloging-in-Publication Data
Hale, Kathleen, 1986–
    Nothing bad is going to happen / Kathleen Hale. — First edition.
    pages cm
    Summary: When sixteen-year-old Kippy finds her boyfriend clinging
to life and everyone in town assumes it was an attempted suicide, she
must find the culprit who wanted him dead, all the while still haunted
by the near-death experience of her last attempt at amateur sleuthing.
    ISBN 978-0-06-221121-7 (hardcover)
    [1. Mystery and detective stories. 2. Love—Fiction.] I. Title.
PZ7.H1352Not 2015   2014047812
[Fic]—dc23   CIP
                                                             AC

Typography by Alicia Mikles
15 16 17 18 19 PC/RRDH 10 9 8 7 6 5 4 3 2 1

First Edition

For my dad

Dear Kippy Bushman,

Nice touch with the PO box return address!
I'm assuming you're trying to keep all of
this a secret from Dom, which is fantastic.
INTELLIGENSIAAAAAAAAA.

No offense but he's a worrier, and we don't
need him to fret about OUR INCREDIBLE
REUNION.

By the way, I was hoping that if you wrote
to me, you'd also send $$$ for the canteen—
BUT PLEASE DON'T FEEL BAD ABOUT IT,
MAYBE NEXT TIME.

ANYWAY.

Kippy, you sound VERY CROSS. Chad
(my counselor here) says it makes sense, given
what happened in October (MURDER, BLOOD,
REVENGE, EXECUTION). He even had me
do PSYCHOLOGICAL ISOMETRICS where I
imagined things from your point of view. In

1

one exercise, I had to talk to an empty chair.

VERY NUEVO FUTURO

Haha!

IT WAS EMBARRASSING!!

How about I share with you <u>FROM MY HEART</u> what I said during that imaginary conversation, is that all right?

MAYBE IT WILL HELP!!

1.) KIPPY, I'M SO SORRY FOR MURDERING YOUR BEST FRIEND.

2.) ALSO FOR DOING IT IN SUCH A VIOLENT WAY, AND WITH SEXUAL UNDERTONES. ☹

3.) By now you know I framed Colt Widdacombe for the whole thing. That probably wasn't fair. (I know this part has nothing to do with us, but maybe you could tell him I'm sorry. <u>TWO BIRDS WITH ONE STONE!!!</u> <u>ONE LETTER FOR TWO VICTIMS!!!</u>)

4.) <u>ANOTHER THING I'M SORRY FOR IS:</u> after they arrested Colt, you started saying the police were on the wrong track <u>AND YOU WERE RIGHT</u> but instead of admitting that, I followed you around in my minivan and reported all your minor legal transgressions (trespassing, loitering, etc.) to the cops—TERRIBLE, JUST TERRIBLE—which got you into LOTS!!! of trouble.

   SORRY FOR INVADING YOUR PRIVACY, Kippy, and for TATTLING ON YOU. I just didn't want to go to prison for the rest of my life, if that makes sense. ☺

5.) Also I'm sorry for accidentally on purpose getting you sent to CLOUDY MEADOWS: A MENTAL ASYLUM. OMG. It felt like a good solution at the time BUT IT WASN'T, KIPPY, IT WAS WRONG, AND I HOPE YOU'RE OKAY, OKAY?? You're probably not. ☹

   I'm sort of getting tired of writing now because my fingers are very DELICATE. (My cellmate keeps complimenting me on them??) But I'll write more TOMORROW.

TOMORROW: AKA TODAY:

6.) Sorry that when you broke into my house because you suspected me (OBVIOUSLY VALID!!!) I chased you with a machete and almost killed you.

THAT WAS MY BAD!!!

I read in the papers that you sustained a fractured skull, multiple lacerations, including a torn earlobe, a broken leg, and a cracked pelvis. ☹ Ouchie-wa-wa. <u>I'M SO SORRY, KIPPY, I GOT CARRIED AWAY.</u>

Does it hurt?

You can tell me.

Is that adequate? Not to sound lazy or unkind about it but I feel like I've done my part.

<u>THE BALL IS IN YOUR COURT.</u>

<u>ALSO, KIPPY,</u> please know that you <u>DO NOT</u> have to write back if you don't want to.

But if you do write back, please send $$$ <u>FOR THE CANTEEN</u>. Or <u>WHATCHAMACALLITS</u>. You know, those candy bars with the chocolate and the crispy stuff and the caramel . . .

Remember: <u>WHATCHAMACALLITS.</u> No other type of candy is desired.

It's just that the food here is terrible, Kippy—<u>OBVIOUSLY NOT</u> something I would say to the cook (Bernard stabbed an inmate last year for disrespecting his huevos rancheros) <u>BUT THE FACT REMAINS!!!</u>

I have to go now. Expect another letter
from me soon.

UNTIL THEN! Until then (echo effect)

Your former neighbor,
Ralph Johnston

PS: thank you for your real cell number.
I know you've changed it _many_ times to avoid
my calls, and I appreciate the gesture. My phone
privileges were recently revoked for reasons
I can't discuss here but I will call ASAP.

I PROMISE I promise

Dear Ralph,

No offense but your letter was absolutely bonkers. We're reading some insane/boring experimental prose poems right now in AP English, and even those are more coherent. Do they have you on medication? If so what kind? Dr. Ferguson prescribed me Ativan "as needed" but it made it hard to read <u>Jane Eyre</u> and I was already behind in school.

And yes, Dr. Ferguson is my psychiatrist— the same Dr. Ferguson from Cloudy Meadows who you thought was corrupt enough to collude with you. (Albus thought he was bad, too, but it just goes to show that crazy people—you + her, not me—think alike.) For your information, Dr. Ferguson resigned from Cloudy Meadows as soon as he found out that I'd been wrongfully admitted there (Thanks, Ralph—"thanks") and now he's helping us build a lawsuit against them. He also doesn't think I'm crazy. He thinks I'm smart. And he's going to do everything he can to get me ready to testify against you (and against Cloudy Meadows, hopefully, if we keep making headway). The trick is to get me past my trauma blah blah blah. Revenge is awesome.

It turns out that people who didn't believe me at first and then saw the light feel superguilty and are even more loyal than they were before. (Jim Steele, for instance, and Dom, too—though Dom's a completely different story. He and I haven't been getting along well lately. Not that it's your business.) Anyway, sometimes accepting someone's help is the same as accepting an apology, and if there's anything I've learned it's that forgiveness is a great way to feel better (BTW I'm not forgiving you. I no longer believe in forgiveness. Your stupid jail counselor might disagree with me on that front, but tell Chad he can go ahead and judge me once he's walked a mile in my bloody shoes—which were, in fact, so bloody following your attack on me that Dom literally had to take them to the incinerator because raccoons kept breaking into our garage to eat the blood.).

Anyway, freedom is nice. I'm writing this

from the passenger seat of Libby Quinn's truck. She's been driving me to my PO box to check for mail from you because she says it's what Jesus would do. She also says she feels bad about the way she treated me "during the Ruth thing." I don't love euphemisms but what can you do. My leg's in a cast and I can't drive.

What else. Dom and Miss Rosa are dating now, not that it's any of your business either. They still spend most nights apart—I think it's because they decided that was better for my development or something. I didn't even realize I liked hanging out with my dad until he started having other plans. Anyway, remember Miss Rosa? She was my anger management instructor after Mom died. We reconnected after you murdered Ruth because I thought that if I sat in on some of her classes I might get an idea of what kind of person could do a thing like that—you know, because all of her students are so violent or whatever. I ended up settling on you as a suspect by accident. It just sort of fell into my lap. So don't get it into your head that I'm some sort of savant detective because the truth is you're just a shitty killer.

Dr. Ferguson says it's natural to feel this angry and that I should let myself feel my feelings, which sounds obvious but doesn't come so easily when you've been taught to be a nice girl all your life. Ultimately revenge doesn't exactly jibe with society's sexist rubric for femininity. I've been reading a lot of Gloria Steinem fan blogs on the subject if you can't tell. Also Dr. Ferguson says I'm right.

I know what you're thinking. "Ooooh, I'm Kippy, I love Dr. Ferguson." Well I do. Sort of. Not like in a romantic way (blegh) but I've been feeling so much better since I started working with him. One day in the hospital I woke up and I was like, "Hm, maybe it's not normal that I have conversations with my dead friend Ruth." But then Dr. Ferguson sat with me and helped me feel better about it without making me feel weird. And that's a hard thing to do because I'm weird. And I don't know. I'm starting over, letting go.

Some days it's like you were never here.

And by the way, I'm still dating Davey and we're really happy together. He still has bad days where he thinks he's under attack (I think I am, too), but the good news is I'm like a sponge in therapy, so I can sort of transfer what I've learned in there to my conversations with Davey, which is helping us both learn how to deal with our PTSD. I don't know why I'm telling you this. I guess no matter how much I hate you there's still this familiarity and it's hard not to revert to that. See how good I am at understanding my behavior?

Lastly I want you to know that I've been writing letters to other people, not just to you. So don't feel special is all I'm saying. I definitely haven't forgiven you.

Love,
Kippy

O HOLY NIGHT

My name is Kippy Bushman, and I'm a crippled interloper, a girl detective in retirement, but also—

"What's that?" Sarah McKetta asks, nodding at the letter in my hands.

We're in the wheelchair van on the way to school, and per usual she is all up in my business.

"A letter from my grandfather," I lie, stuffing it back into my coat pocket.

"Yeah, right," she says. The van's radio is blasting Christmas carols, and between the icy wind whipping through the windows and our driver Mildred's penchant for loud music, I'm starting to freak out. Some days at school the chorus of pencils scratching paper will shrink into silence and beneath the nothingness I'll hear Ralph's heavy footsteps on unseen stairs, with the scrape and thump of a machete dragging behind him. Often I can't tell if the lightning outside is real or remembered.

Dr. Ferguson gives me stacks of books and case reports, all of which prove that people with PTSD can improve, which is good, because personally, I've got a lot of "improving" to do.

"How's it going, ladies?" Mildred shouts, glancing at us in the rearview mirror.

"Pretty bumpy, actually, you incompetent dickhead," McKetta yells back. "Just because I can't feel my fucking legs doesn't mean you have to hit every pothole."

Another dip in the road jostles my bad leg and I shudder, secretly hoping that we get a speeding ticket so that Mildred is forced to slow down. Ever since he took full credit for capturing Ralph, Sheriff Staake has been too busy throwing parades for himself to monitor the local speed limits. Friendship used to be a safe and boring place. But now that the cops are so caught up in their potlucks and their cakewalks—taking advantage of Friendship's goodwill to raise all sorts of money for God knows what—the roads simply aren't safe anymore and petty crime is on the rise.

I do a double take, thinking that I see my former Cloudy Meadows roommate, Albus, on the sidewalk. But it's just a mailbox. My brain knows that Albus is still in the psych ward, but no matter how many times I remind myself of the facts, my mind rebels. I've been "seeing" her a lot lately: riding her bike around town, or in the crowd during a school assembly. It always turns out to be someone else: a little girl with short hair that looks like it's been chopped with kitchen scissors. Some shadow out of the corner of my eye, or in the reflection of a mirror. There'll be a flash of Albus coming around the corner that turns out to be a boy in hunting gear. Once it was a golden retriever. It's normal to get hung up on the people we miss.

Still, you'd think if I were going to be haunted, the ghosts would be of my former best friend, Ruth, (murdered by Ralph), or Mom (murdered by cancer)— someone actually gone, in other words, not some living girl who once helped me escape from a sanatorium. It almost seems like an insult to Ruth and Mom, since I only knew Albus for less than a week. But she's like a song stuck in my head.

Anyway, things didn't exactly turn out so great with my last few friends: Ruth's dead and her photo, now faded by the sun, has been stuck with wires into the shoulder of the highway next to the crop where she was killed; Ralph's awaiting trial in Green Bay for murdering her; and crazy Albus is 100 percent crackers and bananas. So I sort of feel like maybe no friends from now on. It's for other people's own good because maybe I'm bad luck—although actually that's a complete lie, now that I think about it. It's all for me, this *reticence* (SAT vocab word) because I just can't stand to lose anybody anymore. There's nothing left inside me to carve out.

I cringe again. My leg.

McKetta laughs. "How're those bones, cripple?"

"I get my cast off tonight," I mutter. McKetta's been paralyzed from the waist down since trying to fly when she was four, so you'd think she'd be more empathetic about my temporary disability.

She sneers. "Well, it's good to see you dressed up for the occasion."

"These are my most festive pants!" I pull out a stack of laminated flash cards, determined to ignore her. Surely no one will remember I wore these Christmas-tree-print pajama pants yesterday.

"I bet you're studying for some test, aren't you," McKetta says, "like a big old dork banana."

"Dork banana?"

"Yeah, you cunt, a dork banana. Your new name is Cripple the Dork Banana. Fuck you."

"Your hostile words hurt my feelings." Dr. Ferguson is trying to get me to be more confrontational when people say things that I don't like. ("If you can address it in the moment, you'll be less likely to repeat the conversation in your head later.")

I pore over the flash card in my hand, trying to focus. I'm testing myself on sex moves for later. I'll finally be free of my cast after school, so Davey and I decided that tonight's the night. (For sex.)

The front of this card says DONUT THINGAMAJIG.

"How come you study so much anyway?" McKetta asks. "If I had a boyfriend as sexy as yours I'd never waste a single fucking second—"

"Stop." Donut Thingamajig = Eat a donut off your male partner's penis, or "dick," as some people like to call it. I read about this move in *Cosmopolitan* magazine and I was like "Whaaaa . . . ?" *Cosmo* doesn't say exactly what type of donut to use but I think it should be the kind with a hole in the middle. That way, the donut hole mimics the vagina, or "cunt," as McKetta would say. I've also decided I'm going to get two donuts in case one doesn't fit correctly. The bad thing is that I make a lot of crumbs, even when I eat off regular plates, so I will probably make a big mess. Plain donuts will be the easiest to clean up, but they are also, objectively speaking, the worst type of donut.

Also what if I miss the donut and bite Davey by accident? Most plain donuts are flesh colored (well, if you're white like Davey they are—God, I'm being so race normative). The perfect donut for this would be fluorescent orange like those reflective vests that hunters wear so they don't get shot. That way I could protect Davey, because I would know where the donut stops and Davey begins.

One last problem is I don't love donuts. Like, at all. In terms of snacks I would definitely prefer M&M'S, but rules are rules, and M&M'S are probably hard to balance on penises.

"What are you muttering about?" McKetta asks.

I don't know where she gets her confidence from, but I wish I could borrow some. I'm actually pretty body conscious lately, mostly because of the cast, and I'm nervous about achieving my desired sexiness factor tonight because Dr. Clegg said my healed leg is going to look skinny and shriveled, and also kind of grayish, like a corpse leg. (He actually said "Corpse leg." I was like, "Pardon, what did you just say?" And he was like, "Corpse leg.")

"Look at you," she continues, shaking her head. "I mean, no offense but how in the world did you get such a hot boyfriend?" People say this crap all the time to me. All the time.

Also it's crazy how people think they can say "no offense" and magically temper whatever inherently offensive thing they've just said. I glance back at the donut flash card one more time, biting my lip. I still don't totally understand how it will work, but I'm sure that part of it will be instinctive—like, the animal inside of me will rear up and in this gruff voice yell out, "DONUT."

"Davey Fried is a dangerous, erotic man," she continues, ignoring me, her eyes all faraway, "so troubled and dark . . . like a beautiful villain prince." She makes a noise somewhere between a grunt and a sigh. "I bet when he's naked you can see every muscle."

I wrinkle my nose and keep flipping through my flash cards. The next one is superweird and maybe even physically impossible. I remind myself that *Cosmo* is a reputable publication and would never be allowed to publish anything that was made up or unhelpful, so this particular piece of advice must be based on biological facts that a virgin like me simply wouldn't understand.

"I wanna kiss him so bad," McKetta says.

Like everyone, including me, McKetta has a crush on Davey that borders on maniacal. I just wish she wouldn't talk about it to my face. Mildred's the same way. I once caught her crouched outside of the Frieds' house with binoculars.

The truth is, I'm not sure how Davey likes me, either. But the fact is, he does. So I figure it's kind of a waste of time to go around all insecure, asking the universe,

"Why? Why me?" I'd rather ogle my boyfriend's body, sit on his lap, ease my tongue into his mouth until erstwhile dormant parts of my body fill with magma. (*Erstwhile* is one of my SAT vocab words.)

"You little snotbags mocking my driving?" Mildred hollers.

She's paranoid.

"Yeah, we're back here gossiping about you, per usual," McKetta shouts, rolling her eyes. "Your paranoia is completely real, Mildred."

I slap my forehead. It's just like McKetta to provoke her. Last week, McKetta pissed off Mildred so bad that she careened onto the sidewalk. While the van's radio played joyous Christmas songs, Mildred screamed like a banshee for almost an entire carol and a vein popped in her eyeball.

"What'll you do when you don't have any lesser-abled types to drive around?" McKetta adds loudly. "Kill yourself?"

Mildred regards McKetta in the rearview mirror. I notice that one of her eyes is still bloodshot.

"Watch the road," I whisper, more in prayer than conversation. "Please watch the road." A car swerves around us and I brace myself, anticipating a collision. Finally, after all these near misses: death. But after a few achingly long seconds, Mildred lets out a forced, honking laugh, yanking the wheel just in time to avoid the passing car's rear bumper.

"I'll cut off some legs and create more customers," she says gleefully, slapping on her blinker. I close my eyes, unable to watch any longer. This is the last time I'll have to ride in Mildred's van, and we can't get to school fast enough.

"Hey, Kippy," Colt shouts from across the crowded hall, watching as I struggle to get through the bathroom doorway on my crutches. "You need help?"

I shake my head, propping the door open with my elbow and trying to inch through before it closes on me again. After a few failed attempts, Colt jogs over, seemingly oblivious to the way his friends are staring. Everyone in town has been weird around me since Sheriff Staake lied to the press and said that he was responsible for finding "that galdanged murdering psychopath." Of course, he didn't just stop there, he completed the betrayal by telling reporters, "The Bushman girl was just a nutcase who nearly threw me off course, no offense. I'm the hero here. I'm the guy." So now, instead of being "girl detective" or whatever I used to aspire to, I'm that kid who almost got murdered after escaping a psych ward.

"Here we go," Colt says, holding the door. "Come on, Ms. NASCAR." It's the last day of school before winter break, so like most people, he's in a pretty good mood—though the truth is that since "the incident," as Dom calls it, Colt is always pretty cheery around me. In general, people fall into two camps where I'm concerned: 1.) "Kippy is crazy—did you hear that she escaped from a mental ward the night she got all hurt? We better talk a lot about how insane she is, because then it's like she brought it on herself and we can distract ourselves from the randomness of violence and bad things will never happen to us!" or 2.) "Gosh I used to be sort of mean or dismissive to Kippy, and gee she almost died and I'm vaguely Christian, so I better make up for it now by being a total sycophant." Colt falls into the latter group.

"Thank you," I tell him, glancing at the football players who are still watching us with bemused looks on their faces. Granted, Colt genuinely owes me big time; my investigative prowess (or at the very least, my tendency for nosiness/being in the wrong place at the wrong time) basically freed him from jail. We've come a long way since the days when he thought it was funny to call me a prude in the hallway and put deer urine in my car's exhaust system. He and Libby are even covering for me tonight when I go to Davey's. Dom thinks I'm sleeping at Libby's place, and if he calls to talk to her parents, Colt is going to get on the phone and pretend to be her dad. Then they'll call me and I'll call Dom on my cell from Davey's, pretending to be annoyed that he doesn't trust me. It's pretty much foolproof.

"Where are you going, anyway?" Colt asks as the lunch bell rings. "I'll walk with you."

"Mr. Zarwell's to get my anatomy test."

"Colt!" somebody screams, and there's Libby sprinting toward us. I used to have a lot of feelings about how she was so mean to me after Ruth died. But it turns out it's pretty easy to go from enemies to friends. After Libby sent me that weird, passive-aggressive card saying she was dropping all her charges against me, she just started showing up in my hospital room, and sitting there, and talking to me while I drifted in and out of consciousness.

The thing is: a lot of people came to see me, at first— even Diane Sawyer's offices called. But then, all of a sudden, it was just me and Dom and Rosa, and sometimes Libby, and having her around made me feel a lot less claustrophobic. Mostly because Dom only ever wanted to talk about how sorry he was for sending me to Cloudy Meadows, and those conversations always devolved into him yelling about good intentions.

"Oh my Gah," Libby says now, breathless, tugging on

Colt's sweatshirt. They've been hooking up for a month, but they're not "official"—a fact Colt brings up whenever he doesn't want to see her. "Hey, Kippy." She winks at me. "Long time no see." She's alluding to the fact that she drove me to the post office during our morning free period, as soon as Mildred dropped off McKetta and me at the handicapped door, so that I could post my hate mail. Libby's been surprisingly supportive about the fact that I'm trying to channel my anger toward Ralph into something. She's got rage issues, too, she says, so she relates. Mostly she's been in a good mood ever since she mailed off her application to UW–Madison. Her mom and dad and both of her older siblings went there, so she's pretty positive she'll get in—though as far as I know she's gotten straight Cs throughout high school.

God, I sound like Ruth. Why can't I just be preemptively happy for Libby? Probably because deep down I know we're not friends, at least not in a lasting way. I only hang around her and Colt because who else am I going to talk to? Everybody at school thinks I'm damaged goods. Mystery solved.

"Hiya, Soggy Bottom," Colt says, rustling Libby's hair. She quickly fixes it, making a face that's somewhere between a frown and a smile.

"Gross," I mutter. I hate their nicknames for each

other. Not that I have an issue with pet names in general; I call Davey "Lampy" because he lights up my life.

As Libby wriggles her hands into the kangaroo pocket of Colt's sweatshirt, I try not to think about the Colt/McKetta rumors. People are saying he and McKetta have been hooking up again, and McKetta said something weird in the van once, but who even knows. Anyway, I don't feel like I'm obligated to tell Libby about what I heard, since she falls pretty solidly into the "I'm nice to Kippy so that I'll go to heaven" camp. I mean, she has literally told me (many, many times) that the only reason she even talks to me and drives me to the post office to send Ralph hate mail is because it's what "Gah" would want.

"Ew, why are you looking at me like that?" she asks now. "Are you gonna puke?"

"Are you going to the Frostbite Challenge?" Colt asks, pulling Libby's hands out of his pocket.

The Frostbite Challenge is this competition on Christmas Eve where anyone who wants to can pay a fee, get a gigantic slab of ice, and try to make something pretty out of it using any tools at their disposal, besides migrant workers. One of the wealthier families once hired an entire group of contractors from Mexico to come and carve for them, and everyone agreed it was cheating. Also, none of the contractors were mentally, emotionally, or physically prepared for the Wisconsin cold. They all showed up in denim jackets and two of them went home with full-blown pneumonia.

"Yeah, I'm going," I say. "Davey's making a sculpture this year, so—"

"What's he making?" Libby asks, all lightning quick. I can hear the competitiveness in her voice. She and her dad have won the Frostbite Challenge three years in a row, and she's always on the lookout for potential rivals. Last year they did a perfect ten-point buck and this year they're doing Jesus on the cross (they're really religious, hence why Libby never says "God").

"It's just, like, a big heart, actually," I say, grinning. "A big heart by a big, big-hearted boy."

She nods, satisfied that Davey won't beat her.

"I think my dad and I are going to make a square this year," Colt says. "Last year we tried to do a sphere, but it was too complicated."

"Hey, did you guys see someone painted over all the speed limit signs on Main Street?" I ask. "Mildred, like, whizzed by them today and we almost died."

"That was me." Colt grins. "Hey, maybe you should call 1-800-TEENTIP." In an effort to crack down on petty larceny, the Friendship police set up this thing called the Teenage Tip Line—aka, 1-800-TEENTIP—which relies on the notion that younger residents who are more "with it" will call in and rat on their hoodlum peers. So far, the tip line has mostly been used to prank people, and the most recent victim was Dom; the kids at Friendship Middle School where he's a counselor called and said he kept human bones in his desk. Staake and his minions showed up a few hours later with their sirens blaring and essentially turned his office upside down looking for skeletons. Obviously they found nothing and meanwhile there were three car accidents on Main Street.

"I've actually called the tip line about speeding," I tell them quietly, "countless times, and to no avail."

Colt and Libby laugh, thinking I'm joking.

I frown, picking lint off my crotch. "Whoever runs it must recognize my voice or something and delete the messages. I don't exactly have the most sterling reputation around here, if you didn't know."

"You're so paranoid," Colt says, rolling his eyes. "Look at how many people like you." He flicks a finger at my leg cast, which is covered in squiggly signatures. After a while people at school ran out of space and started signing my arms and stuff—like, my actual skin—and since I couldn't always get away fast enough, I had to start wearing a sign around my neck that said, *Please don't autograph me; I'm a human being with feelings.*

"You must be psyched to get it off," Colt says, shaking the hair out of his eyes. "How long has it been?"

"Forever." I glance at the clock. Only two more hours before Dr. Clegg.

Libby's eyes are wide. "What if they take the cast off and your leg is gone?"

I shake my head.

"I've heard sometimes the leg is gone," she insists.

"Libby—"

The intercom crackles above our heads and Principal Hannycack starts reading the lunch menu.

"Pizza," Colt screams as soon as the main course is announced. "Pizza, pizza!"

Libby and I watch him sprint toward the cafeteria.

"I wonder if he'll get into college," she says, cocking her head.

Something flashes in my peripheral vision and at first I think it's Albus, but it's the bubbler. I roll my eyes around in their sockets, trying to fix them.

Libby jabs me lightly on the shoulder. "FYI, Kippy, I know you asked me to get you a scrunchie, and I actually found one in our attic, in this box marked, like, *1997*, but I decided against bringing it, because it's, like, deeply against my fashion principles to contribute something so ugly to such a special occasion." I actually asked Libby to root around for a scrunchie because of this other tip I read in *Cosmo*. But I keep that to myself. She glances anxiously at my pajama pants and the Christmas stocking sock that Dom slipped over the bottom of my cast to keep my toes warm. "What are you wearing tonight?"

I smile, grateful to think about something other than anthropomorphized drinking fountains. I rattle off my outfit: one sexy cream slip, and everything else the color of a red velvet cupcake. I describe each accoutrement in so much detail that eventually she cuts me off.

"Ew, what does 'festive hat' mean?"

I shrug. "It's, like, floppy."

"Don't forget to pray first. Also you should shave your legs, your armpits, and your arms. Davey will expect some sort of effort, you know."

"My arms? I didn't read anything about that in *Cosmo*."

She looks alarmed. "Yes, Kippy, girls shave their arms—and you have fuzzy arms, no offense. Also, don't forget to use Summer's Eve on your hoo hah. It's a douching product."

I chuckle heartily. "I'm not doing that."

"You should douche, Kippy. Your hoo hah's precious. It's supposed to taste like a flower."

"First of all, humans don't eat flowers—"

"Dinosaurs ate flowers."

"—and it's called a vagina. Wait, you believe in dinosaurs? I thought the whole idea of Jesus was at odds with dinosaurs?"

Before she can answer, a football player called Dollar Dan runs by and slaps me on the ass. "Hey, Crazy Kippy," he says, winking at me.

"Stop it, Dan!" Libby snaps. He's been doing stuff like this ever since I got back to school. He keeps saying that I should tell him the next time I'm getting sent to Cloudy Meadows so that he can do something crazy and get sent there, too, and we can finally be alone. No matter how many times I explain to him that I'm not going back—that it was all a big mistake to begin with—he doesn't seem to get it.

Dan grins. "You know it doesn't matter if you get your precious daddy to shut down Cloudy Meadows, right?" he shoots back. "Everybody still knows it's where you belong." He leans in so I can smell his bacon breath. "Where *we* belong."

Libby shoves him. "Back off, Dollar Dickwad. Stop trying to make this like some insane indie romance."

I swallow, wondering how he found out about the lawsuit we're building against Cloudy Meadows. Dom and Rosa and Jim Steele have been working on it with Dr.

Ferguson for weeks now. But so far it's all been secret. They're trying to prove that I'm not the only person who's suffered unethical treatment at the hands of Cloudy Meadows nurses. I've been really careful about not mentioning it to other people.

"Also I told you that stuff about the lawsuit in confidence," Libby says.

"Libby!"

"I want her," he says, nodding at me. "When're you gonna get rid of that boyfriend, anyway? Or do you want me to get rid of him for you?" He cracks his knuckles.

"If you come near my boyfriend, I'll kill you." It's a weird, gravelly voice, and it takes me a second to realize that it's mine.

I shake my head hard, trying to get whatever that was out of me.

"Come on, Kippy," Dan says, whining now. "Talk to me. I just wanna know you, baby. Tell me about what it was like in there, with all those wild, crazy girls. Better yet, tell me about Ralph." Dollar Dan is as creepily obsessed with Ralph as he is with me. It makes my skin crawl. I cross my arms and shake my head, feeling queasy.

"How close were you guys, exactly?" he continues. "Did he ever see you in a nightgown or whatever?"

Libby shoves him so hard he lands on his butt.

"What the fuck, bitch?" he shrieks, scrambling to his feet.

I smile at Libby, my ambivalence toward her suddenly evaporating. Not everyone's great at keeping secrets, for one thing, and people were going to find out about our lawsuit anyway. Plus, something that's cool about Libby is that even though she takes a lot of shit from Colt, he's pretty much the only person she takes shit from. It's nice to have someone stand up for me.

"Girls are crazy," Dollar Dan yells to no one. "Dollar Dan rules!" He jogs off.

"It's so gross that people call him Dollar Dan," I mutter.

"Yeah, because he's got nipples the size of silver dollars," Libby says. "He's always getting drunk and showing everyone at parties—it's a total deformity, but he's a guy so people think it's awesome. Like when Nate Silver took a crapola the size of a guinea pig and everyone lined up outside the boy's bathroom like it was Six Flags Great America. If you or me had Dollar Dan's reputation, they'd call us salami tits and nobody would ask us to a dance, ever. Meanwhile he's some fatso but so many girls kiss up to him that he thinks he's cool to touch butts."

I shake my head, awestruck. Libby might think that casts make legs disappear, but she just nailed so concisely a complete double standard that I've never been able to articulate. Suddenly part of me wants to blurt out the McKetta rumors, because even though it's just gossip Libby deserves to know that Colt is most likely cheating on her the way he cheats on everyone—although maybe it would be gentler to simply lend her the Gloria Steinem book from my backpack? Yes. With Gloria's help, Libby could come to understand that her insensitive nonboyfriend's hold on her is part of a complex system of oppression—and then the two of us could see eye to eye, and become best friends, and start a blog about our shared beliefs.

"You're making that pukey face again," she says.

Who am I kidding? Libby and I are never going to start a blog. She probably doesn't even like me—she talked to Dollar Dan about me and my lawsuit, for goodness' sake. I need to get a grip—to remember Ruth and Ralph, and how everyone I get close to either dies or betrays me. It might sound like narcissism, but it's also based on cold, hard facts. I have the tendency to get obsessed with the wrong people, and I need to protect myself from that.

"Personally I think Dollar Dan seems nice," I lie, and hobble away, feigning interest in today's lunch.

HEAR WHAT I HEAR

"Kippy, I'm so sorry for killing your best friend," Ralph says, standing over me. Albus blinks from across the room, frozen on her Cloudy Meadows standard-issue twin bed, and I am screaming, but screams do nothing, noise never has—and now his hands are on my leg, clenching hard, and the pain in my knee is like lightning.

"Pickle," Ralph says. "Pickle."

Why is he—

"Pickle?"

I blink, sucking in air. Dom's hand is on my shinbone. Behind him, through the living room window, I see snow falling gently on the lawn.

"It's just a dream," he says. "You fell asleep on the couch."

My eyes dart wildly, still expecting to see Albus or Ralph

crouched in a corner. I don't usually dream about them both at once. To tell the truth, I don't usually dream about Albus at all, which is weird since I think about her a lot. Ever since Dr. Ferguson resigned from Cloudy Meadows on my behalf I've had lots of guilty feelings about her. He's helping us but she's still stuck inside, being forced to down pills and walk through life in a drugged-out haze. Dom says the case we build against Cloudy Meadows will help Albus, too. But in the meantime part of me sometimes wishes Dr. Ferguson still worked there. If only to look out for her.

"Should I get the Ativan?" Dom asks. He's always offering me the stuff Dr. Ferguson prescribed, but I'm like, How can a pill help with nightmares if it just puts you to sleep, leading to more nightmares?

"Honey?"

I shake my head. My back is slick with sweat.

"You conked out after school is all," he says. "Are you ready to get that cast off?"

I let him pull me up. Fear is sort of my default these days, so we're used to this routine by now: I come home from school tired from not sleeping due to nightmares, and then I take a nap and have a nightmare. Dr. Ferguson tries to put a positive spin on it all by saying that hyper-awareness and hair-trigger panic are part of my newly honed survival instinct.

*　*　*

As we enter the hospital through the automatic doors, I gaze up at the fluorescent lights buzzing overhead and blink, reminding myself that I'm supposed to be excited. My cast is coming off. I have big plans tonight. This is the start of the rest of my life.

The nurse leads us to the small white room divided down the center by a curtain, and the first thing I do is yank it back, expecting Albus to be there, but it's just another empty examining table.

"Honey?" Dom asks, an anxious note in his voice. He wants to know why the heck I'm tearing back curtains. I wish he wouldn't worry so much.

"I just wanted to see . . . if that table . . . looked more comfy."

He nods, seeming to accept this, and holds my crutches while I hoist myself onto the examining table. The little saw for cutting patients out of casts is affixed to the wall in some kind of holster, and the curlicue cord is plugged into the floor. The blade is silver and catches the overhead lights in a way that makes my mouth water. Not like I'm hungry but like I might throw up. I close my eyes. Everything smells like bleach.

"Well, here we go, you little Evel Knievel," Dr. Clegg says, walking in and rapping his knuckles on the plaster.

"It won't hurt even a little—I promise." But he's promised that before.

"Okay," I squeak.

He plucks the cast cutter off the wall and revs it a couple of times. I watch the tiny blade glint under the white lights and taste metal.

"What's your name?" Dom asks, trying to get me to focus. "Spell your name for me—you're excited about this, Kippy, remember?"

But I'm already gone.

"Hello?" Dr. Ferguson says. "Ferguson speaking."

"Hey, Dr. Ferguson. It's me, Kippy."

"Hello, you Kippy." He pauses. "Everything okay?"

"I thought you said I could call you on this number whenever."

"I did. It's just that when you call me on my home phone, I assume it's urgent—especially when I'm going to see you at your house in . . . forty-five minutes."

"Yeah, but we're going to be surrounded by people then and I wanted to talk to you in private. I'm calling from the bathroom at the hospital. I got my cast off."

"Congratulations!"

"Yeah. Thanks. But I had another one of those fainting spells, and I was just wondering—"

"You blacked out? When? Are you all right?"

"Yeah, fine—I was already lying down. But I just wanted to check with you about sex . . . things. What I mean is: Am I going to flashback during sex?"

Silence.

"I mean, I know I want to have sex. But now I'm worried I'll have a flashback or whatever in the very middle, only in flagrante—like, completely naked."

"I'm familiar with the term *in flagrante*."

"What if I'm flailing around all flashbacky and I ruin the whole moment?" I look down at my new walking cast. It's an ugly black boot. "Not to mention, what if I associate sex with trauma forever after that, and can never get it right? What then?"

"Let me get this straight," he says.

"Okay."

"You called to see if I think you're going to faint during sex tonight."

"Uh-huh."

"But otherwise you're okay."

"Yep."

"No panic attacks?"

"No."

"And how is your overall mood?"

"Ugh, Dr. Ferguson, no offense but I don't have time

for your whole suicide-checklist rigmarole."

He sighs. "What were the exact circumstances surrounding today's fainting spell?"

"Getting my cast cut off. I saw the blade they were using and just conked out."

"Because . . ."

"Because it reminded me of that night. Ralph's machete. Like, bam, I was back in his house. I could smell his musty closet all over again. I could basically feel the vibrations of his footsteps on the stairs."

"Flashbacks are completely normal, Kippy, given what you've been through—"

"I know," I blurt. "But am I going to have one tonight?"

"You blacked out today because you were reminded of a near-death experience that centered almost entirely around intense physical pain," he says gently. "Correct?"

"So?"

"So are you afraid that Davey will hurt you?"

"No. Davey only ever makes me so happy that I want to be immortal."

"And are you afraid that sex will hurt you?"

I scoff. "I've been wearing super-jumbo tampons for, like, four whole years."

It's quiet for a second.

"Dr. Ferguson?"

"I can't make any promises," he says finally. "But in my professional opinion it seems unlikely—given that you have never associated Davey with Ralph, or vice versa, or confused the two—I simply think—"

"Yay!" I yell, and hang up.

Text from Kippy (mobile):
It's off!!! Now I'm stretched out in the backseat of Dom's car sipping ginger ale because I fainted. I have to wear this ugly boot/walking cast thing for a while, but you can take it off very easily just by un-Velcroing it. (Write that down **hint hint**!!!)
Anyway I hope you're still coming to the "barbecue" tonight. Or as Dom likes to say, "BBQ." Isn't that annoying? It's like, hello, it has exactly the same number of syllables, so it doesn't save you any time to say, and also it's not even technically a barbecue, we're just eating hot dogs and burgers in the kitchen. There's, like, three feet of snow outside.

Friendship, WI, is weird, huh?

Text from Kippy (mobile):
So are you coming?

Text from Kippy (mobile):
Hello?

Text from Kippy (mobile):
Davey?

Text from Kippy (mobile):
Helloooo? Lampyyyy?

Text from Davey (mobile):
whoa, whoa, hold up. My phone only accepts texts up to
160 characters so I'm reading this in chunks. . . .

Text from Kippy (mobile):
Sorry! I'm turning into Dom. All of his texts are like
manifestos.

Text from Davey (mobile):
haha yeah but I love ur manifestos!

Text from Kippy (mobile):
Eeeeeeeeee!

Text from Davey (mobile):
One sec still reading . . .

Text from Davey (mobile):
ok, so the bbq thing, I sorta wanna clean up 4 when we
"talk on the phone" later. Ok if I don't come?

Text from Kippy (mobile):
 No that's fine! I don't even wanna go! (PS I love when
you communicate in code.)

Text from Davey (mobile):
oh u mean . . . . when I say . . . .

Text from Davey (mobile):
"talk on the phone"

Text from Davey (mobile):
?

Text from Kippy (mobile):
Exactly.

Text from Davey (mobile):
"talk on the phone"

Text from Davey (mobile):
"talk on the phone"

Text from Davey (mobile):
"talk on the phone"

Text from Kippy (mobile):
YES!!

Text from Davey (mobile):
KNO WHAT I'M SAYIN

Text from Kippy (mobile):
YOU'RE SO COOL LAMPY

Text from Davey (mobile):
no ur cool

Text from Kippy (mobile):
Okay we're home.

Text from Davey (mobile):
ok

Text from Kippy (mobile):
TTYL!

Text from Davey (mobile):

yeah . . . . talk to u later . . . .

Text from Kippy (mobile):
Huh?

Text from Davey (mobile):
"ON THE PHONE"

Text from Kippy (mobile):
oh!!!! RIGHT!

Text from Davey (mobile):
xo

Text from Kippy (mobile):
faints

Text from Davey (mobile):
catches u

Text from Kippy (mobile):
<3 <3 <3 bye for real

Text from Davey (mobile):
bye beautiful

Miss Rosa plants her elbows on the kitchen table, bows her head, and says a quick prayer in Polish. Dr. Ferguson fiddles with his Santa napkin, watching her uneasily, like he thinks she might be casting a spell instead of talking to God. Meanwhile Dom drums his fingers on the red-and-green Christmas tablecloth, salivating at the pile of hot dogs sweating on a platter in the middle of the table, and Jim Steele stares blatantly at his watch. I guess none of us is particularly religious. Also, we don't speak Polish. So we have no idea what Rosa is currently saying.

Eventually Rosa looks up, blinking at us through the hot-dog steam.

"I am saying no more evil, please," she explains, translating.

Jim Steele shakes his head, scowling in disbelief. "What an absolutely hideous-sounding language."

She ignores him. "I tell Jesus, 'Kippy's cast? Gone. Cloudy Meadows? Almost gone. Now? Nothing bad is going to happen, please.'" She passes me a charred veggie burger patty. "Special food for Kippy, who is hating hot dogs."

I smile at her. "Thanks. I don't hate them, it's just . . . I don't know." I stop myself before I can blurt out that I'm having sex tonight, and eating phallic foodstuffs at a time like this seems a little *much*. Metaphorically speaking.

Rosa thumps the table and I scream, nearly dropping the imitation meat. It's embarrassing how easily I startle. Two weeks ago I opened my eyes to see Dom clutching his mouth and bleeding—apparently he snuck up on me while I was dozing off after school and I socked him in the face.

"Have you been doing your exercises, Kippy?" Dom asks. I made the mistake of telling him about the relaxation exercises Dr. Ferguson suggested, and now he won't shut up about it. Basically Dr. Ferguson wants me to imagine myself on the beach, digging my feet into the sand, anchoring myself someplace peaceful. Or to hum a song I know and focus on the lyrics—something joyful, preferably. Pinching myself can also fend off fainting, he says. But the problem is, I can't predict when somebody will drop a tray in the cafeteria, or when a storm will hit. I can't control the random stuff that fuels my anxiety, so it's not like I can really prepare for it, can I?

"Yeah," I lie. "I'm fine." I'm starting to think that sanity and lying to make people happy are basically the same thing.

"Oh baby Kippy," Rosa whispers. "Sweet animal in human skin." She's been getting way more affectionate with me since she and Dom started dating, but the language barrier can make it weird. Sometimes she calls me Mud Dumpling.

"You are my sugar lump," she says now, nodding at me sternly. "Later I will hug your body."

I sigh. Back when she taught the Non-Violent Communication Group, Miss Rosa wouldn't let herself touch anyone in case she accidentally hurt them—and I kind of preferred that, honestly. Now she holds my father on her lap during breakfast.

I yelp at the sound of Dom smacking the serving spoon against his plate to get the potato salad off, and everybody turns to stare at me again. "You're like a girl possessed," Jim mutters. You'd think he could be a little more sensitive.

Dom shakes his head. "Kippy, I really think we should reconsider medication—"

"Get off her nuts about it," Rosa hisses, losing her temper unexpectedly. "Look her face, how red, you embarrass!" She's prone to little outbursts, but I notice more and more that they're usually on my behalf.

"Yeah," I mutter. "You embarrass. Besides, I tried that stuff and I hated it. I couldn't study on it."

"Everybody talk, talk, talk, Mud Dumpling," Rosa

fumes, switching her glare to Dr. Ferguson. "All these men saying they know. Who knows? She fine. Is normal for scream all the time after murder. What you think, she should be happy rainbows with milkflies in her eyes?"

"Milkflies?" Jim asks, looking sickened.

"What you call?" Rosa purses her lips. "How do you say . . . colored tiny birds with dairy name?"

"Butterflies!" I say, feeling like I've won a quiz.

She grins, pointing at me with her hot dog. "Yes." Her eyes narrow and the smile slips into a scowl, directed firmly at Dom. "She is not happy just because she is girl."

Everyone stares at her. It's like I'm the only one who gets what she means, and personally I think she's right. People might talk about how Davey's a hermit, but nobody questions his right to be a little messed up. He's, like, earned his right to PTSD, or something. Whereas I'm supposed to bounce back and be all sugar and spice so people can stop feeling guilty about me. And how is that even possible when I was never sugar and spice to begin with?

Dom forces a smile. "Rosa, come on, what did we talk about?"

She frowns. "Yes, fine. I am not the mama." She gnaws sadly on her hot dog.

I want to reassure her, but I don't know what to say.

Dom is always getting on her case for being overinvolved with me, whatever that means. It's pretty hypocritical, in my opinion, when you consider that Dom's the most overinvolved dad in the whole world.

"Tell us about your day, Kippy. Did anything happen at school?" Dr. Ferguson asks, breaking the silence.

I think of Dollar Dan grabbing my ass. "No," I mumble, gnawing on my rubbery veggie burger. "People were mostly preoccupied with Christmas break and the Frostbite Challenge, and stuff."

"To winter break," Dr. Ferguson says, raising his beer.

Everybody clinks and drinks. Toasting isn't superfun for me, since I'm the only one without beer (Dom makes me drink milk with dinner; he says it's good for my bones, even though that's been proven false by science websites), but everyone's too caught up in their own celebration to notice how little I want to join in.

"Where's Davey tonight, Kippy?" Jim asks, exhaling after a long draw on his Miller High Life.

"He's not feeling well," I mumble.

"Seems like he doesn't feel well an awful lot," Jim says, raising an eyebrow at Dr. Ferguson, who ignores him. Dom ignores him, too, but that's because he dislikes me dating Davey more than anyone. Dr. Ferguson's the only one who even gives Davey a chance—well, him and Rosa.

Rosa acts very sneaky around Davey, mumbling and narrowing her eyes, sort of dancing back and forth. She can be very hyperactive around people she likes.

Rosa thumps the table. "More toasts," she says.

"Well, okay, how about to the Cloudy Meadows lawsuit," Dom says proudly. "If all goes well, we should be going public with it by New Year's." He beams at me. Dom, Miss Rosa, Jim Steele, and Dr. Ferguson have all teamed up to go after the institution that, as Dom puts it, "Almost ate my baby alive." They've decided that if they can prove unethical handling of one case (mine), they can potentially set free a bunch of other girls who were never meant to be there in the first place. Dr. Ferguson doesn't work there anymore out of principle. But the administrators at Cloudy Meadows don't know that—they think he was simply old enough to retire, which he was. He earned his pension a while ago. So he still has the friendly ear of the powers that be, and hears a lot of interesting things when they go out for beers or bowling or whatever. For instance, someone on the board recently took Dr. Ferguson to play darts and let it slip that "a hundred more bodies in the looney bin" would buy him and his wife a nice summer cabin. Ferguson also still has access to files of patients he saw there—who knows why. It's probably not legal that he took them, but the fact that he did might help other girls get out. The files are stored away in his house somewhere. Jim's already started going through them, compiling evidence. He found out that my friend Albus— aka Adele Botkins—got brought into Cloudy Meadows when she was only eleven because her stepmother didn't like the way she sang to herself and occasionally climbed the furniture to make "forts." That tidbit made me cry. "You've got to get her out," I said to Dr. Ferguson, "her especially, more than anybody else—she's just a kid." The craziest part is that Cloudy Meadows is such a messed up and disorganized institution that nobody even seems to notice that the files are missing.

I glance at Dom, who's still grinning at me like an idiot, waiting for me to say how great it is, this thing he's doing—how great it is for *me,* specifically. Dom seems to think that if he works hard enough to shut down Cloudy Meadows, it will absolve him of all guilt, and he and I won't have to talk anymore about the fact that he stuck me there unfairly.

"Yeah," I finally say. "Fantastic."

Dr. Ferguson flashes me a sheepish, knowing smile. He's aware of my feelings toward Dom on this subject. I actually think a big part of the reason I started trusting Dr. Ferguson again is because he's so frank about stuff. I mean, at least Dr. Ferguson said sorry, and acknowledged that he messed up by admitting me to Cloudy Meadows in the first place. And it wasn't even really his fault—it was Dom's. And those nurses. They were the ones putting drugs in the food. And Ralph was the one who lied so Dr. Ferguson wouldn't know that the only reason I got sent there was because of one corrupt cop and an impressionable father.

"That psych ward needed to be looked at," Dom says, shaking his head like the world is on his shoulders. "Yessirree bob."

"It's a shit hole," Jim Steele says with his mouth full, glancing warily at Dr. Ferguson. "No offense, Will."

Dr. Ferguson shrugs. "I wouldn't be here if I didn't agree."

"Well, we're going to protect you when we go public with all of this, I'll tell you that much," Dom says.

"A lot'll hinge on your testimony, Kippy," Jim chimes in, mouth still chomping his meat.

"Don't pressure her," Dom says gently.

Dr. Ferguson smiles. "Kippy and I are working hard on that. Pretty soon she'll be able to handle it."

Yeah, I think, *maybe I'll be able to talk about it without fainting.* "It's fine," I snap. "I'm not a China doll."

"We free the girls?" Rosa grumbles. She raises her fork and zigzags it through the air. "Set them loose!"

Dr. Ferguson nods. "As for the few who do need to be there, they'll be set up with the right facilities. Better facilities."

"But the real reason we got together tonight . . ." Dom beams at me again. "The real reason . . ."

It's like he's waiting for me to finish the sentence.

I stare at him. "Because I got my cast off?"

Dr. Ferguson clears his throat and Rosa pats her greasy lips with a napkin. They're all doing these weird Mona Lisa smiles. For a second I'm afraid they're going to tell me that I'm going back to Cloudy Meadows—but no, they would never do that.

"Do you wanna tell her, Jim?" Dom asks.

Jim shakes his head, but even he looks excited. "Go ahead, old man. It was your idea."

Dom's smile stretches to the point where I can hardly take it. Everyone's looking at me expectantly. It's too much attention. I feel hot and itchy.

"What?" I shout.

"Well," Dom says, eyes sparkling. "If everything goes the way we think it will—that is, if Cloudy Meadows gets shut down—we're gonna offer classes to help some of the longer-term patients ease back into civilian life." He nods proudly. "We're calling the program Team Kippy."

I look away. First of all, I'd prefer they didn't name

anything after me—people in town talk enough as it is. Second, I hate when Dom paints all this like I should be thanking him.

"Maybe Davey could use some of those services," Dr. Ferguson says gently, and my stomach lurches. Oof. I was *just* thinking about how Dr. Ferguson was one of the only people on my side when it comes to Davey. What's he going to do next? Tell the whole table that I'm doing it tonight?

"Davey's fine," I reply firmly, giving him a look. The truth is that ever since Ruth died, Davey's parents have been off on these grief retreats, leaving him alone in the house where he just sits around playing video games. People around town either have major crushes on him (cases in point: Mildred and McKetta) or else they stigmatize him and make it like he's creepy because he never leaves his house—which isn't even true. He comes over here all the time.

"I've been telling her, Will, believe me," Dom says, raising his eyebrows. "I say, 'That boyfriend of yours has got a screw loose and by God it's the last thing you need—'"

"The only reason you think any of that is because he's older than me."

It's quiet except for Rosa slurping on her beer. "I like Davey," she says.

"He should get a job," Dom grumbles.

"What is he supposed to do?" I ask, frustrated. "Work at the local Buck Fleet? That would be great, wouldn't it? He could make minimum wage and hang out with killers all day. He's only been home from Afghanistan for, like, two months. He can't just jump into a job."

Dom puffs air out of his nose, all judgmentally. "He didn't just *come home*, Kippy. The army *kicked him out*."

"*Special Ops* kicked him out, a bunch of high-profile assholes who wouldn't let him come back for his own sister's funeral. And they didn't really leave him any choice, did they? So what if he shot off his finger! It was the only way to get home and say 'Bye' to Ruth before she decomposed."

Everybody's staring at me again.

"Language," Dom says finally.

"Which part?"

"When you said 'A-holes.'"

"Anyway, his biggest problem in the beginning was his drinking, and he's been sober since I got out of the hospital," I mumble, playing with my food. "He's fine."

"To fine!" Miss Rosa says eagerly. Everyone around the table tentatively raises their glasses, anticipating another outburst from me, I guess. My leg is starting to hurt.

"You all right, Kippy?" Dr. Ferguson asks.

I nod shakily, trying to picture the beach and dig my toes in imaginary sand like we practiced. I concentrate on the dull ache in my once-fractured pelvis. I've got pins and needles in my femur, but Dr. Clegg says those should go away—and anyway it shouldn't matter for tonight, since most of the things I'm planning to do sex-wise involve lying down.

"To free girls," I proclaim, spilling some of my milk as I lift my glass skyward, and everyone cheers.

After Dom and Rosa and Jim and Dr. Ferguson are all drunk enough for me to sneak out quietly, I limp upstairs to change into my outfit, and to mentally prepare for tonight's adventure. (In other words, I review the flash cards a couple of times.) I throw a long trench coat on over my negligee and belt it tight, peering down the stairs to make sure the coast is clear. Libby's driving me to Davey's, and I want to get outside before Dom grills me about my "sleepover with girls—yes, Dom, lots and lots of girls, all girls." He's basically a human lie detector.

I take a step toward the door and the floor creaks beneath my weight. The drunken laughter in the kitchen stops.

"Dammit," I whisper.

"Wait! We want hugs!" Rosa yells.

"Oh no." I grapple with the doorknob, but it's too late.

"How come your calves are bare?" Jim Steele asks, crossing the foyer. "And what's with the box? Are those donuts?"

"You'll catch your death, Kippy!" Dom exclaims, filing in behind him, wide-eyed at the sight of my bare legs.

Dr. Ferguson shuffles through the doorway, his face red from beer. He sees the look on my face and glances warily at Dom. "Er, why don't we all go sit down? I brought cupcakes."

"At least let me get you some winter leggings," Dom says, crossing the room to pluck at my flimsy coat. "And what's with this . . . rain jacket thing? What are you, Mary Tyler Moore in autumn? It's below zero outside."

"No!" I bark, clutching it to my neck, but the coat isn't buttoned, just belted, and before I can catch it, it's fallen open from all Dom's prodding.

Rosa's eyes widen. Dr. Ferguson clears his throat uncomfortably, and Jim Steele laughs out loud. I'm standing there cold and exposed, wearing Mom's old cream negligee in front of everyone.

"Kippy Bushman," Dom sputters, in this sad, old voice. "What are you up to?" Something clicks and his eyes turn mean. "You're going to Davey's, aren't you?" He's literally frothing at the mouth now, wiping spit from his trembling lip. "I know what—I know what you're up to!" I can't even look at him.

"I'm sixteen," I say quietly. It's all I can think to say. Libby's tires crunch on the snowy driveway. She honks her horn.

His lip curls. "You little—"

"Dommy," Rosa says, waving him over. But he storms past her through the kitchen. I hear the garage door open, and watch through the window as he weaves the Subaru perilously around Libby's trunk.

"You go, Kippy," Dr. Ferguson says. "We'll talk to him when he gets back. He'll cool off."

"Ho, boy." Jim Steele grunts and heads back into the kitchen. Presumably to drink more.

Miss Rosa waddles over and gives me a hug. "Have fun at sleepover," she says. I can't tell if she caught what just happened or not.

I hug her back and hold on for a while, ignoring Libby's honking.

When I climb into Libby's front seat she grabs the donuts from me and tosses them in back.

"Hey," I yell. "Careful. There's jelly ones in there."

"Gross. Hey, what the heck was up with your dad just now, anyway? Drunk driving or something?"

"He's crazy." It doesn't seem nice to say, especially given

how much I hate being called that myself. But it's the first thing that springs to mind. "We fight all the time now."

"Ugh, I remember when that started with my dad," Libby mutters, careening down the salted road so fast I have to press a palm against the ceiling to avoid getting thrown into the door. "It's all about sex and stuff. It's totally gross and weird. He and I had a great relationship until I grew tits and then everything sucked. Pretty much the only time we talk is when he gets out the chainsaws for us to do our yearly ice sculpture." She glances at me. "You'll get used to it."

"That's depressing."

Within a few minutes, our headlights illuminate Davey's garage door. Eight p.m., right on time. "I've got an idea," Libby says, cranking her truck into park. She turns toward me, smiling wide. "How about you let me do your hair? You look like a blond thing of cotton candy, and it's not pretty."

"Has anyone ever told you your voice is like a verbal eye roll?"

"My dad tells me that *constantly*." She shakes her head. "Dads. They're so *sassy*." She reaches over and before I know it she's somehow shaped my long, unbrushed hair into a perfect bun. She claps her hands until I put the festive red hat back on. Then she frowns.

I open my coat to show her my negligee. "Can you believe I found this in Dom's cedar chest of Mom's old stuff? Isn't it perfect?"

She crinkles her nose. "Wait, isn't your mom dead?"

"Yes."

"So you're wearing . . . like . . . dead clothes?"

"Clothes don't die." I look down at the negligee. It's really pretty, embroidered with little black flowers at the hem. When I was little, Dom hated how I'd go through that cedar chest.

"Well, it's nice, I guess, but *that* thing is ugly," Libby says, wincing at my walking cast. She makes the word *ugly* last forever. "I'll text you in the morning to see when I should pick you up."

"Thanks. What are you and Colt doing tonight?"

She shrugs. "Probably playing Xbox or something dumb."

"Oh. Cool." I swing out of the car. "Oops, donuts." I swing back in and reach for them.

"You think tonight will be romantic?" I ask.

"Xbox?"

"No!"

"Oh . . . right! Your thing."

Icy air curls up the bottom of my coat and I shiver, slamming the door.

"Kippy," she says, rolling down the passenger window. "You okay?"

"Duh." I nod, check my reflection in the rearview mirror, and adjust my red hat, feeling disappointed. I want to be perfect.

"Kippy? Look at me."

"Yeah?"

"Don't be nervous. At a certain point you're not in control."

"What do you mean?"

"It's like a basket toss, okay? It's like ballet." She nods rapidly, smiling. "You've got to practice it a couple of times before you land it—then it's muscle memory—but the first few tries it's in Gah's hands. Not that I would know, obviously, because I don't believe in sex before marriage. No offense." The window suctions closed.

As she pulls away I can hear the dogs barking outside. Davey must have put them out to pee and forgot to let them in again.

"C'mere, guys," I yell, whistling, and they bound around the house toward me, yapping like crazy—really barking their heads off. "What's wrong with you?" I limp up the walkway to the screen door. Warm air from inside the house coils through the mesh, colliding with the icy wind like smoke.

I ring the doorbell and wait a second, my teeth chattering. "Hey, Lampy, I'm here!" I call. There's music on inside so he probably can't hear me. I let myself in and leave the dogs out—they're really hyper for some reason and I don't want them jumping up and tearing my negligee or something.

"Davey?" I slough off my trench, licking my teeth to make sure there's no lipstick. The dogs are barking so shrilly that I'm starting to get a headache. I hear footsteps and look up to see a shadowy figure crouched at the end of the hall on all fours.

The box of donuts pops open as it hits the ground, launching a few onto the carpet. My legs wobble and I sink to my knees on a raspberry jam–filled, cream-glazed one, spurting jelly on my legs.

I force myself to stand up. My heartbeat slows to a slight rattle. "Jesus, Davey, you scared the shit out of me."

It's too big of an occasion, I decide, to worry about the mess that looks like blood.

I force myself to smile, turning in my negligee. "What do you think?"

He's gone.

"Is this some kind of sex thing?" I yell.

Something streaks past the living room window—Albus?

No, I remind myself. Not real.

But was the shadow man real?

I hobble down the hallway, telling myself the figure in the hallway was just Davey—just fooling around—we're both nervous, that's all—then I round the corner to the living room and see a man splayed out on the carpet, surrounded by beer cans and pill bottles and shards of glass from the coffee table. There's vomit covering half his face, oozing frothily from his mouth. His leg twitches and I am somewhere above myself watching me scream, rolling Davey over and wiping at my boyfriend's face, trying to help him breathe.

EMT REPORT

PATIENT: FRIED, DAVID, 20 YEARS OLD, MALE

PAST MEDICAL HISTORY: PARTIAL
AMPUTATION OF RIGHT INDEX FINGER AND
PTSD

ALLERGIES: NONE

MEDICATIONS: XANAX, AS NEEDED

BREATHING QUALITY: ABNORMAL

CENTRAL BODY COLOR: ABNORMAL

FINGERS, LIPS, AND FEET WERE PURPLE FROM
PROLONGED LACK OF OXYGEN. PUPILS DID NOT
RESPOND TO LIGHT. UPON ARRIVAL, FRIED
WAS BREATHING AS HIS COMPANION (SEE
BELOW) WAS ABLE TO CONDUCT CPR USING
VERBAL INSTRUCTIONS FROM DISPATCHER.
FRIED WAS RUSHED TO HOSPITAL AND FOUND
COMATOSE. EVENTS HAVE BEEN RULED
ATTEMPTED SUICIDE.

***PATIENT #2

KIPPY BUSHMAN WAS FOUND ON SCENE.
SHERIFF BOB STAAKE AGREED TO DRIVE HER
TO THE HOSPITAL IN A NONOFFICIAL MANNER
(NO ARREST).

"Message sent today, December 21, at 8:32 p.m.:

'Kippy Bushman? Uh, hello there. This is Ralph Johnston. I hoped to speak to you, but you're not picking up, so now I am leaving you a message! I got my phone privileges back, which is very, very exciting. It's the little things in here. One day at a time, as they say.

'Anyhoo, I am calling you to see if you received my present? I sent you a present, Kippy, and it's a big one. You betcha. Don't be scared, okay?

'This is going to be fun.'

"End of message. To delete this message press seven, to save it press—"

MERRY GENTLEMEN

"Suicides are hard," Staake said. "Davey was an okay boy."

"*Is* an okay boy—*is*, present tense—and I already told you, he wasn't trying to hurt himself." I am attempting to breathe through the tightness in my chest. My voice is hoarse from screaming and there's a space under my ribs that seems to swallow itself whenever I think of Davey or the fact that he might not wake up. We've been here for almost thirty minutes, and there's still no update from the doctors except that it's critical. I can still see his face—blue around the mouth, puke everywhere—

"All right then, *attempted* suicide," Staake says, making it sound like I'm being some kind of language snob.

"Davey was happy," I say, trying to stay calm. I clench my

teeth. The fluorescent lights in the hospital's waiting room make me feel like a bug roasting underneath a magnifying glass. "*Is* happy. Tonight we were . . . he was excited to . . ." I search for the words. "He was excited to hang out."

Staake smirks knowingly. I ignore him.

"Somebody was there," I continue, rubbing my chest. I'm pretty sure my heart might explode. "Somebody hurt him and I refuse to leave this waiting room until they check his hands for signs of struggle."

"Geeze Louise Bushman—"

"Two months ago you called Mrs. Klitch's murder a suicide, and you didn't even check her hands. There were cuts everywhere—"

"What exactly were you thinking of achieving in this getup, anyway?" he snaps, nodding at the hem of my negligee.

"That is a huge digression," I whisper, feeling icy. I can smell the beer on his breath.

My stomach sinks. This man can't help me. He never could. Even if he had any brain cells, he'd still be too drunk to follow what I'm trying to tell him.

I wrap my trench coat tighter around myself. The heat is cranked up and it's boiling in here. But I wish I had a million more layers.

Maybe I can simplify it for him. "You've got to call

Green Bay Correctional, Sheriff Staake. You've got to make sure Ralph's still locked up."

"Oh right—because he called you and alluded to some special gift, huh?"

"He said he sent me a package! 'A present,' he said—but there wasn't any mail for me today. I checked the PO box—"

"The what?"

I look at my lap, not wanting to admit to my continued correspondence with Ralph.

"If he left you such a crystal-clear murder message, then why won'tcha play it for me?"

"I already told you, I pressed a button by accident and deleted it."

He chuckles, wafting more rancid beer breath my way. "That's handy."

"Sheriff Staake—" My voice catches and I stop short. My chest hurts so much that I can barely talk. The pain is sharp enough that tears are blurring my vision.

"Okay, okay," he says gently, thumping my back. "Calm down, why don'tcha—I don't wanna make you all hysterical."

I groan. The thumping feels nice, actually. "You gotta get out there," I plead, swiping at my face and trying to breathe normally. I've had attacks before and that's what

Dr. Ferguson always says: "Breathe. This is your brain, not your body—breathe." But what about when your brain is telling you there's a killer loose, and nobody is listening because they think your brain mixes up what's physical and real with what's most feared? Who do you call then? "There was someone at the house." My voice is scratchy. "I saw them—Well, I saw a shadow, but—"

"Honey, I checked that house up and down, and everything I found points straight to suicide," he says.

I glare at him until he rolls his eyes. "Okay, okay." He holds up his hands. "I'll say it again: *attempted* suicide. You girls get so hyper about plain old words, it baffles me. Every little phrase has to be as perfect as one of your embroidery projects."

"What?"

He wags a finger in my face. "All I'm saying is, hopefully tonight will teach you a lesson about God and law. Sexy pajamas might look cute on the models, but in real life they get you into trouble."

"Sheriff Staake, please focus. If I'm right we're all in extreme danger."

"Well now, Kippy Bushman, Miss Sassy, I for one think you should hold up with your outlandish theories and your general make-believe mentality. You're having one of those stress responses, is all. You probably need to talk to that psychiatrist I've heard you see." He pulls a lollipop out of his coat and hands it to me. "Go on, forget your diet a second. I know you girls love your sweets just as much as your princesses and flying ponies and your big imaginations. You think you'll sit there looking cute, and then: a man will come."

"Oh my God." I slump in my seat, feeling vaguely jealous of Davey that he gets to be asleep and temporarily apart from the rest of this weird bullshit world.

Then I snap out of it and hate myself for ever thinking that.

"You ready to leave yet?" Staake asks.

"I told you I'm not going until I find out what's happening with Davey." I look around for a nurse or a security guard or somebody to talk to, but the waiting room is empty except for us.

"They're not going to tell you anything, Bushman, because you're not his family."

I grit my teeth. "I'm staying. Whoever did this might come back. I need to protect him."

He leans in so close that the smell of his breath makes me want to puke. "We're talking about Davey Fried here, the same boy who shot off his own finger to get out of the war, no offense. Now don't get me wrong, I respect him for going out there and doing what he did for our country. I don't hold the same grudges others do, no sir. I don't tell myself, 'Oh well, he shouldn't've come home that way, what a phony.' No sir, he sacrificed two years for us before he hurt himself, and I don't discount that. But, Kippy, honey, I found an empty forty-eight pack in the house. The boy was drunk. He took a ton of pills—"

"It was a setup," I plead. "He wouldn't hurt himself."

"He's in a coma," Staake says, but he's not talking to me. I follow his gaze to Dr. Ferguson standing near the magazine rack.

"You go ahead," he says to Staake. "I'll drive her home."

I blink through tears. "I can't believe you actually called my psychiatrist."

"Oh, that's who this is," Staake says, saluting Dr. Ferguson. "Don't let her get too hysterical, Doctor." He slaps his knees and stands up, groaning from the effort. "Take care now."

I wipe my eyes with my sleeve as Dr. Ferguson sits down next to me. "That guy doesn't have such a fantastic bedside manner, huh?" he says.

"Nope," I mutter. "He also doesn't believe me about what I saw."

"What did you see?"

I roll my eyes. "You probably won't believe me, either."

"Is that a certainty or a concern?"

"Both." I snatch the tissue he offers. "I saw . . . a figure . . . a shadow of a guy . . . I think—no, I definitely did." I nod vehemently, snuffling. "He was in Davey's house when I showed up. And, well, this is going to sound crazy, but I think it was Ralph. At first I thought it was just a burglar—I don't know, maybe someone broke in and beat Davey up, took money or something, and made it look like a suicide. But there was money left out and a pair of Mrs. Fried's nice earrings on the counter, and no one took that . . . so . . ." I lick my lips. "And then Ralph called, and said all this weird stuff about did I get his present—"

"Ralph?" He sounds shocked.

"Yeah."

"Are you sure?"

"Of course I'm sure. He left a message."

"Can you play it for me?"

"Ugh, why does everyone"—I dig my fists into my eyes until I see stars—"I hate this."

"Okay," he says softly, like he's afraid I might explode.

"Don't be so nice—don't treat me like I'm crazy."

"Okay," he says again in the same tone. "Here's the thing, though, Kippy—I'm not trying to challenge you, but the shadowy guy you've just described sounds remarkably similar to the figure in the flashbacks you and I have talked about."

"I know."

"Why don't I take you home? I can come by your place tomorrow evening for an impromptu session."

"When?" I wipe my eyes.

"I can swing by around seven."

The cold air doesn't shock me when I leave the hospital. I'm not sure anything can shock me at this point. As the streetlights and darkened yards whip past my window, I think I see Albus a zillion times—which I guess should worry me about myself, but the thing is, you can have post-traumatic stress disorder and still be self-aware. Most people don't know that but it's true. I know what's real and what isn't. And I know what I saw tonight.

By the time we get to my house I've calmed down enough to feel what I can only describe as vaguely cantankerous about the fact that there's a homicidal maniac out there and I'm the one person who wants to deal with it. I mean, here I am, just some girl trying to get boned, and instead I have to hunt down a killer. *Again.*

"Can you get in okay?" Dr. Ferguson asks, easing the car into park.

"Please don't infantilize me."

"Kippy, you just got your cast off. There's snow outside."

I push open the passenger door and plant my boot on the salty blacktop. It's supposed to hurt this early on to put your full weight on the injured leg. But I don't care.

I trudge up the walkway past our Christmas decorations. Before I can get my key in the door, Dom swings it open and just stands there, staring at me like some petulant cross-dresser. He's wearing the pink bathrobe that Miss Rosa got him for his birthday, and the face cream he got himself for his birthday, and he looks shiny and furious. He obviously didn't get all that rage out of his system when he careened out of the driveway earlier.

"Look, I know I'm still wearing Mom's . . . thing . . . which implies certain . . . things," I say, pulling my coat tight over the negligee. "But I'm your kid, and I'm tired, and my boyfriend's in a coma, so maybe we could just not fight right now? You basically already served me right when you refused to pick me up from the hospital— which, by the way, was a pretty low blow."

"I can't deal with this," he says, spinning on his heel, all haughty.

"Are you at least going to ask if I'm okay?"

"I'm going to sleep."

"You waited up all this time just so you could make some dramatic gesture of rejection?" I watch him climb the stairs and feel completely tongue-tied. He thinks something happened that didn't even happen, and he's acting like the thing that did happen didn't happen—and since when does virginity have anything to do with fatherhood anyway?

"I didn't even have sex," I call after him.

His bedroom door slams.

I blink away angry tears. I lock the front door but I still don't feel safe. "Oof," I mutter, scrolling shakily through the contacts on my phone. Due to my no-new-friends policy, there's hardly anyone to call—well, there's one person.

"Rosa? Yeah, it's me, Mud Dumpling," I say when she answers. "Will you come pick me up?"

As soon as we step foot into Rosa's pint-sized (or, I guess, Rosa-sized) brick house—and before I can even fully explain what I'm pretty sure is going on (conspiracy, murderers on the loose, etc.) —we hear Rosa's landline ringing off the hook.

"Hello?" she barks into the phone. "What? Oh, hello, Kitten."

Ew. It's Dom. She calls him Kitten even though compared to her he looks like a wooly mammoth. He's probably calling to continue whatever weird Dad breakdown he's having, and to ask what the hell's going on, and where the hell I am.

I wave my hands around and make a face, indicating that I don't want to talk to him.

"Quiet yourself, Dominic," she says, nodding in my direction as if to reassure me that she's handling it. "I leave my cellular at home—is fine, why is all this yelling? Okay, so you call many times, so? I am here now. Yes, of course she is here. I already tell you that I pick her up . . . Well, yes you say is not okay, but then I come anyway . . . Because I am woman and Kippy is woman. Too much boys in her life right now I think and it is bad for her. Is late and she is tired, no more madness—oh? Uh-huh."

I can hear him whining through the earpiece. Probably telling her to stay out of our family affairs. He wants to have her around all the time, but he's always saying he doesn't want her involved in my "upbringing." As if I'm going to confuse her with my real mom.

The only thing they ever argue about is me, and I guess I should feel guilty, but it's kind of nice, having the attention. Not to mention having someone on my side.

Rosa rolls her eyes at me, and I answer with an eye roll of my own.

"Here is question, Dominic," she snaps, her double chin appearing and disappearing with each violent nod. "Are you small child? Yes, is serious question, Dom—Oh, okay . . . so . . . you . . . you are not tiny baby child? Does this mean you are grown-up man, maybe?"

She winks at me. Meanwhile, Dom's response, though indistinct, is very loud—so loud that it rattles the phone in her hand.

She presses it harder against her face, listening to him rant.

"What is he saying?" I whisper. I've never seen them fight like this.

"Is crazy," she whispers back, covering the receiver.

"Dom?" she says, going back to the phone call. "Yes I listen. What? . . . 'Statutory rape'? How . . . oh." She smiles, listening to Dom's frantic explanation. "Oh yes, yes—I see. Is sex thing. In Poland we don't have this. When man is older, we say to the girl, *'Gratulacje.'* It is meaning, 'Ah, how good for you child, congratulations. He die soon, cooking is not so long for you. *Gratulacje!'* Then we dance . . . What? Yes, I remember patriarchy conversation. Was boring. Rosa slept long time after."

Whoa. Dom knows the word *patriarchy*?

"Hey," Rosa continues, sounding a little defensive, "older man is nice for girl. What is problem if he dies and she goes free like bird from cage? Is feminism, correct?"

I furtively shake my head. Child brides are not feminism. But no one could say that Miss Rosa isn't trying.

Rosa grunts, pressing the phone even harder into her round face, as if proximity might clue her in to what Dom means.

"What?" I whisper.

She holds up a hand for me to wait, letting him talk awhile. "So what is wrong with being slut?" she says finally.

"Wait." I look around. "Me?"

"In Poland we say *szmata*," she says to Dom. "Is also word for rag, for cleaning floor. Rag for cleaning floor is very useful. Agh!" She yanks the phone away from her ear like she's been electrocuted. Dom's tinny voice honks furiously from the earpiece.

"Why are you screaming?" Rosa yells, still holding the phone at arm's length. "Now you are yelling too much so my brain is hurting—there is pain on my ears with your baby screams—"

She hangs up, looking exhausted, and shakes her head at me.

"He pleases me sex," she says. "Is good for to remember when I want killing him."

"You sound like Yoda." Also, ew.

"Yes!" She grins. "*Yoga* is also good for making calm. Down dog and child's pose." She kisses her fingers with a flourish and collapses onto the floor in a tiny ball. "Your muscles, they like it."

"Did you get my present, Kippy? Hey, don't be a bitch," Ralph is saying. "I won't hurt you, so long as you're nice."

The machete in his hand starts to vibrate, emitting a buzzing sound, like an electric shaver.

"Well, this is odd," he says, laughing at the shivering blade. I force myself to start laughing with him, hoping he won't hurt me. But then his eyes change.

Bzz. Bzz. Bzz.

I jolt awake, screaming to the sound of my phone buzzing on the coffee table. The vibrations send it skittering across the glass until it lands with a soft plunk on the carpet. At first I'm relieved that the nightmare is over, but then I remember where I am and why: It's the first official day of winter break, and instead of being sprawled out on Davey's futon—my important body parts draped elegantly with sheets like in some beautiful rom com—I'm scrunched up on Miss Rosa's too-short sofa, drenched with sweat, stuffed into a pair of her teensy pajamas that I'm pretty sure I just ripped from thrashing awake.

Bzz. Bzz. Bzz

I scan the floor for my phone and see a note taped to one of the coffee table legs.

HELLO MY PEBBLE.
I GO GROCERY. ALSO TALK FEELINGS TO DOM.
SOUP IS ON!

ROSA

I taught her the phrase *soup's on* a few weeks ago, and I think she loves it because she uses it even when she isn't cooking—like when we're waiting in the drive-through line at McDonald's, or when she's about to enter a room. Or when the Packers are winning.

I toss the note on the table, pick up my phone, and survey the weapons spread out on the floor. When I told Rosa about the shadowy figure at Davey's house, she not only believed me but said that we should arm ourselves. She locked all the doors and brought out a whole bag of knives and stuff that I didn't know she had. Then she taught me how to build some basic booby traps, including trip wires.

Somehow, instead of feeling more freaked out by all the shiny blades, I actually felt safe—finally—to the point where I didn't even need to sleep in the same bed with

Rosa, which was a huge relief, mostly because she snores like a bear.

Anyway, it turns out I feel most at ease when I'm in an environment where my heightened anxiety feels appropriate. Like in a room full of loaded weapons. I should mention that to Dr. Ferguson tonight, at our impromptu session. I wonder if it's a thing.

My phone starts buzzing again in my hand. I don't recognize the number. "Hello?"

"Hey, girrrrl," Libby says. "How in the glory heck was last night?"

"Oh." I stupidly didn't put her in my phone because of my no-new-friends policy. If I had, I definitely would have ignored this call.

"Did you like it or did you love it? Do you need me to bring over an ice pack for your hoo hah? I've only texted you a billion times."

"Things didn't go as planned," I mumble. Across the room, Mom's negligee is draped over a chair.

"What happened?" Libby asks, lowering her voice. "Was his you-know-what too big?"

"What? No—"

"Oh Gah!" she shouts. "It wasn't too small, was it?"

I slap my forehead and take a deep breath. "Libby, are you sitting down?"

"I'm on the treadmill," she says.

"You're not even breathing hard."

"I'm an athlete," she huffs. "I have, like, terrific stamina."

"Davey's in a coma," I say, just to get it out. "When I showed up at his house last night he was unconscious and there were pills everywhere and Staake says that he drank forty-eight beers, but he didn't, also there was an intruder in the house and I think Ralph was involved because he left me a weird voice mail but no one believes me—"

There's a crashing sound in the background.

"Libby?"

"I fell off the treadmill," she calls, sounding far-away. "One sec, I gotta find my phone. Oh my Gah!" she exclaims, her voice loud again. "Are you okay?"

"Are *you* okay? You just flew off a treadmill."

"Whatever, my body's built for speed. Did the police come?"

"Just Staake."

"Ew. Did he check the house?"

"Yes. He didn't see anyone." I tell her about the voice mail from Ralph.

"But the PO box was empty yesterday," she says.

"I know."

"This is really weird."

Rosa and Libby. That's two people who believe me now. "Also, thanks for not immediately assuming he tried to kill himself. That's what everyone else is saying, but it isn't true."

Libby's quiet. "Duh," she says finally.

"I was thinking maybe I should go to the hospital? I could call them but I feel like I'd be more likely to get the full scoop in person. I just want to know how he's doing."

"Double duh."

"I was there last night, obviously, but they wouldn't let me in because Davey was in critical condition, and, like, ICU policy dictates family only."

"I hate it."

"I know." I roll my eyes. "His family's not even here yet—they're on their way back from one of their grief retreats. But the point is I'm not allowed to see him yet, which—"

"Um, I'm pretty sure that we can get around that," she says.

"What do you mean?"

"You'll see. I'll pick you up in fifteen. Get dressed."

I glance at the clock. It's only nine a.m. Rosa won't be home with lunch for at least another few hours. "I actually don't have any clothes, is the thing—"

"YES. The answer is yes. I've been waiting forever to

dress you. A fashion transformation is what Gah wants for you, Kippy, believe me. What a blessed day."

"I'm not really in the mood for that." Ruth used to give me makeovers all the time and they made me feel superawkward. The last thing I want to do right now is enact some kind of movie makeover montage. "Just basic stuff. Please? Like . . . long underwear that actually fits would be great. Miss Rosa's so tiny. And . . . I don't know. Maybe a snowsuit? With bling on it? That might be nice. Maybe I'm asking for too much."

"I am, like, soooo disappointed right now I can't even express it to you," she says, and hangs up the phone.

THE HOLLY AND THE IVY

The ICU was basically vacant last night but now it's surging with activity. Apparently there was a pileup on the interstate by my house. The magazine rack in the waiting room is empty and the chairs are filled with strangely calm relatives, all slurping coffee out of Styrofoam cups and mumbling about black ice and Christmas miracles. "It could have been so much worse," somebody says, smiling at us, thinking Libby and I are related to someone from the crash. "Luckily it's just broken bones."

My phone buzzes: a text from Jim Steele awkwardly asking if I need anything because "suicide's the worst." Unsure how to respond, I text him back an emoji of a bear.

"You ready?" Libby whispers, cocking her head really intensely. "When I say go, we go."

I look down at the velour zip-up hoodie she convinced me to wear. It says *JESUS RULES* across the front in glitter. ("I told you I'm agnostic, right?" I said when she handed it to me. "One soul at a time," Libby responded, smiling.) I conceded to put it on *under* the snowsuit she brought me because today it's a record-setting cold of thirty-five below with the wind chill.

"Kathy!" a doctor shouts, sticking his head through the door. "I need you to help me hold this kid down—he's a thrasher!" The nurse gets up from behind her desk, scuttling off.

"Perfect," Libby says, tugging me through the door to the ICU. "Come on." She insisted on lugging in her gigantic purse with us. When I reached into it looking for ChapStick, she got really angry and told me not to touch her stuff. She's being really weird.

"What do you even keep in there?" I ask, digging my heels into the floor to stop her from pulling me through the door marked *EMERGENCY.* "Wait, stop, what if an alarm goes off? We don't have permission." I glance over my shoulder but nobody's watching—they're all too busy commiserating over close calls.

"Kippy." She sighs, edging around a gurney. "When you look like me, you don't need permission."

It's true that Libby's good at getting what she wants.

She hardly ever works for anything and a lot of people say the only reason she's passing high school is because teachers can't keep their eyes off her cleavage, and feel bad about it, and worry about getting sued. I've overheard enough conversations to that extent.

"What if she claims sexual harassment?" Mr. Bender, the biology teacher, asked one day when I was accidentally on purpose eavesdropping near the teachers' lounge. (*Libby* sounds a lot like *Kippy*, so I thought I heard my name—though it quickly became clear that they were not talking about me.)

"She looks like a model from one of those sex magazines, don'tcha know. I feel like I've gotta pass her."

"Give her that C," Mr. Hannycack responded. "Don't quote me on it, Frank, but I sure think it's best to avoid any hubbub, you betcha."

"I don't know how to put this," Mr. Bender continued, "but she could say I'd been looking and she wouldn't be lying."

"Join the club, Frank. Anyone with eyes would look."

Come to think of it, Libby grew religious around the time she grew boobs. As soon as they got gigantic at the tender age of ten, she started all these Jesus committees— I guess to ward off the dirty rumors that were already spreading about her, despite her age, and based solely on her bra size. Then she began aggressively proselytizing to anyone she hadn't seen in church, which mainly included Ruth, who was Jewish, and me, because I had trouble going back there after burying Mom. Libby would yell at me to show up more often, or else risk hellfire. She still encourages me to come with her on Sundays, though she's nicer about it now. And honestly, I have to admit I'm drawn to the idea, if only because I want so badly to believe in something other than myself. And I know it helps other people to gaze heavenward when folks around them start dying. But I feel like if God were something real, I'd know it by now. My mom is dead, and I've had neighbors pass away, and now Ruth is gone, and so far it doesn't feel like there are all these new angels in heaven smiling down on me, keeping me all warm and protected. As far as I can tell, they've disappeared.

"You need info, right?" Libby asks now, unzipping her tight hoodie to reveal about an inch of cleavage. "Fine. I'm gonna walk around until I find the right idiot."

"You're going to seduce an orderly?" I hiss.

"Not all the way!"

"You don't have to debase yourself on my account! We'll get information somehow—"

"Geeze Louise, honey, enough with all your gender crap. I'm just using what Gah gave me, and I'm only gonna stand there talking. It doesn't take much else. Now let's split up." She shakes her head at my outfit. "You go look for Davey. No offense but this isn't gonna work if you're standing next to me. You look like a gigantic toddler."

I gaze down at the snowsuit she brought me; it's a vibrant shade of purple and covered in black polka dots. Libby said she found it in one of her mom's attic boxes labeled *1987*. All that matters to me is that I'm warm—well, too warm now, actually.

I unzip the snowsuit like Libby did with her hoodie. "Is that better?"

She shakes her head, so I tie the arms around my waist, exposing the full phrase *JESUS RULES*. "How about this?"

"Perfect—now go," she says, shoving me. "Find your BF. And if anyone sees you, pretend you're crazy and wandered in by accident."

I duck around the corner, bristling slightly at the word *crazy*, and crouch behind a bubbler. A doctor walks across the hall, clutching a stethoscope around her neck, and disappears into a dark room, shutting the door behind her. There aren't many places on this floor that Davey could be, so searching for him shouldn't be too hard.

I scamper across the hall and start checking the charts hanging outside the doors.

Albus, the first one reads.

I press my eyelids and look again.

It says, *Erica Sussman*.

I decide not to dwell on the mistake for too long. The point is that it's not Davey.

Eleanor Harbeck.

Nope.

Christopher Hernandez.

Nope.

"What are you doing here?" somebody asks.

I spin around and gulp. A man in a white coat is glaring at me. "Libby?" I yell.

She careens around the corner, snow boots squeaking on the floor, boobs bouncing, and arrives at my side breathless.

"Hello," she tells the doctor, leaning casually against a wall-mounted dispenser of hand sanitizer.

"I like your coat," I hear her say as I escape to check more charts.

Stephanie Georgopolis.

Nope.

David Fried.

Bingo!

There's a note on the front of his chart: *Attempted suicide using aspirin. State: comatose.* I tear off that part and shove it in my pocket before opening the door.

"Davey?" I call quietly. This morning I read online that people in comas can probably hear you.

I pull back the curtain and there he is. Just a few days ago I was lying stretched out on our couch with my leg on a pillow, and the front door slammed and there was Davey, tugging off his coat in the entryway. Dom was in the kitchen cooking sausages. He preferred Davey to come to our place, rather than the other way around.

"Hey," I said.

His eyes trailed from my red lipstick to my red nail polish. Snowflakes were caught in his hair. "Does it hurt today?" he asked.

He meant my leg and in response I lied, shaking my head. The John Williams *Home Alone* soundtrack was playing in the other room—Dom's and my favorite mash-up of Christmas carols.

"This one's my favorite," Davey said, lowering himself onto the couch. I lifted my legs and he slid under them, warming his icy hands on my toes.

"Who's your favorite?" I said. "I'm your favorite?"

"Well yeah." He laughed. "But also this song."

"'O Holy Night'? You haven't turned all Christian on me, have you?"

"No, it's just . . . You know that part where they sing, 'Fall on your knees, O hear the angel voices'?"

"Sure," I said. "They sing it during that part in *Home Alone* where the so-called bad guy becomes, like, a human being. It's objectively the most powerful moment in the song."

"I love it." He leaned back. "I dunno, it just always reminds me that sometimes you have to listen to the crazy stuff inside your head."

"You mean like . . . listen to your gut."

"Yeah, sure, if that's what you wanna call it."

Just then Miss Rosa came barreling down the stairs in one of her crazy Christmas sweaters and he slid away from me—not that she'd care, really. Whenever Dom caught Davey and me together, he'd scream, "Stop it with the sugar!" But if Miss Rosa saw us, she'd just gurgle like a pigeon, and get all wide-eyed, shouting, "YES! VERY GOOD! I LIKE!" which I guess made Davey uncomfortable for other reasons.

"Soup is on!" she yelled. I could smell the venison sausages smoking in the kitchen. "O Holy Night" was still blaring in the other room, and I found myself focusing on the lyrics, waiting for the part he'd mentioned.

"A thrill of hope, a weary world rejoices, for yonder breaks a new and glorious morn."

"I get excited every time I see you," I told him.

"Same," he said.

That was two days ago. Now he's lying here, slack-jawed, with all these tubes sticking out of him, hooked up to so many machines. His face is pale and waxy but his hair looks the same, soft and dark and thick—and there's about a day's worth of stubble on his face, which I guess means everything's still working.

"Psst, Kippy!"

The curtain swings open behind me. "We've gotta go," Libby says. "Sorry."

"Just one sec." I reach for Davey's hand—it feels the same, all callused and huge compared to mine—and my skin reacts the way it usually does: like it's got a million nerve endings connected to every part of my body. His fingers are cold but not, like, dead cold.

"Come on," Libby says, tugging on the sleeve of my hoodie. "I told that doctor to get me one of his business cards so we could be boyfriend-girlfriend and he'll be looking for me soon."

"I'm not leaving yet," I tell her.

"Okay, listen," she says, putting her hands on her hips. "I was going to wait until we were in the car to tell you this but—" She looks around.

"What?"

"Davey's blood-alcohol level was zero," she whispers.

"Which means you were right all along. Somebody planted those cans there—which means whoever's saying you made up the burglar person can go screw themselves." She glances at the ceiling. "Sorry, Gah, but it's true."

I want to scream with joy and relief—Davey wasn't drinking; I'm not crazy.

"Now come on!" she says, glancing at the door.

There's a hubbub in the hallway and I tell myself it's probably better to follow her lead and get out of here. If the hospital calls the cops then I'll have to face Sheriff Staake again. And I don't know if I can handle another run-in with him.

"Okay," I say, letting her push me toward the door. I glance over my shoulder to take one last look at Davey before the curtain falls back into place. "Libby, how come you're being so nice?"

"Huh?" Libby scrunches up her nose, looking taken aback. "What do you mean?"

"It's just, I don't know. . . . Remember in middle school, you used to call me Kippy Little Tits?"

"Yeah, well, remember what my nickname was? Donkey Tits."

"But I didn't call you that."

She pushes open the door to the waiting room and

leads me through the noisy crowd. The parents of the kids who got into the car accident are talking over one another in raucous prayer.

Libby shoves me in what I'm sure she thinks is a friendly way, but her cheerleading muscles make it sort of rough. "None of us were at our best in middle school, right?"

"I guess so."

I follow her to her truck in a daze, zipping up my snowsuit and pulling down my balaclava to avoid the freeze. Whatever Libby's reasons are—guilt or Gah, and what's the difference really—it's nice to have a wingman. I need the help, but the trick will be to keep my composure and not get attached to her. I have the tendency for overexcitement, and a history of mixing business with pleasure. During my investigation into Ruth's murder, Davey was my wingman, and we all know how that turned out.

My phone buzzes again. Word about Davey has clearly spread, and multiple people have posted suicide hotline numbers on my Facebook wall. I quickly delete the posts.

"Should we call the police?" I ask. "About the blood-alcohol thingy?"

"You tell me," she says. "You're the one who had to deal with Sheriff Drunk last night. Do you really think he'll help?" It's a rhetorical question.

My phone rings in my pocket and I answer it reflexively.

"Hello?"

"This is a call from the Green Bay Correctional Facility," an automated voice says, loudly enough for Libby to hear and get wide-eyed.

"That's Ralph, right?" she says. "Ask him what the heck he meant by sending you a present—go ahead, Kippy, talk to him. I'm right here."

"Kippy?" Ralph says.

"Hi," I stutter.

"Ask him," Libby mouths.

"Ralph, what did you mean in your message last night? I never got a package from you."

He doesn't respond, just giggles a little.

"Ralph?"

"Did you get my letter about sending bars? Whatchamacallit bars, specifically."

"I did, but, Ralph, tell me what you meant about the present."

"I need a lawyer, Kippy. I need a very good lawyer—an expensive one. Luckily I'm very rich now."

"What are you talking about?"

He yawns. "There's a storage facility outside of town where my collectibles are being stored while I'm in jail.

That's the entirety of my money: hundreds of thousands of dollars worth of coveted *Star Wars* paraphernalia. When I cash it in I might be forced to send you another little present."

"Is someone auctioning your stuff for you or something?" I ask, ignoring the threat.

He laughs again, a weird, high-pitched giggle, like a girl's. "I've got to go, Kippy. I just wanted to call and hear your voice—please tell Davey I say hi."

My chest feels cold.

"What did he say?" Libby asks as I hang up. "Are you okay? You're making that barfy face again."

"He just kept laughing," I tell her. "Then he told me to say hi to Davey for him." I swallow hard.

She looks scared. "Maybe we should go back to Rosa's."

"No. If we're going to do this, we have to do it right," I say, feeling my heart race. "We've got to gather evidence." I take a deep breath. "We've got to return to the scene of the crime."

Dear Ralph,

When I called you back just now I got an operator lady who said that inmates can make calls but can't receive them. Perfect. Now I have to wait for you to call again. I guess that's what you want.

I'm writing this from the passenger seat of Libby's car, which has basically become my office, and if you were standing in the middle of the road right now and I were driving, I'd run you over.

This is what I've figured out so far: You called me from jail, so I know you didn't do this with your own hands. You got someone to help you, and knowing you, you want to make some kind of game out of watching me find out who it is. You probably think you're being nice, don't you, letting me play detective again? You're sick but so am I. And lucky for me I found someone even weirder than me to help: Libby's not just driving me around anymore, she's helping me figure out <u>what the hell is going on</u>.

Well, mostly she's still driving. Right now

she's busy singing along to Beyoncé, which is kind of ironic when you consider the fact that the lyrics are mostly about self-empowerment and Libby's stuck catering to Colt's every whim. I mean, we're not really friends or anything—she's sort of just my driver—but if we were, I'd definitely tell her about the rumors that Colt's hooking up with Sarah McKetta.

Dr. Ferguson once told me that victims have a tendency to recreate the circumstances that made them victims to begin with. Not because they want to get hurt, but because it's familiar. I don't think that's what these letters are.

Ugh! It's hard not to get all contemplative and casual and basically revert to my old self when I'm writing to you. That's the real reason I got in touch with you in the first place, if I'm being honest with myself. I mean, yeah, I wanted to express my anger, and to make you feel bad, so I wrote you hate mail. But mostly I feel like I've unraveled into this completely different person. It's hard not to feel nostalgic for when things were simpler.

I miss Davey. I'm afraid he's a vegetable.
Libby's a pretty good wingman but—well,
you've met her. Her boobs are bigger than
her brain and she's so used to getting what
she wants, she thinks the answers are gonna
fall straight from heaven.

What am I doing! You don't deserve
to hear about any of this! I wish I could
have reached through the phone lines and
strangled you. I'm not sending this one.

Love,
Kippy

WONDER AS I WANDER

Outside Davey's house, there's a little girl's bike on its side in the snow, which is weird because he doesn't have any particularly young neighbors that I know of. I could have sworn it wasn't there when we showed up last night, but it *was* dark at the time, so who knows.

"Weird," I mutter, before following Libby through the unlocked front door. Inside Pasta Batman and Marco Baseball are barking like crazy and lunging for our crotches. The heat is blasting, making the smell of stale beer even stronger. I should have locked up when Sheriff Staake made me leave last night, but to be fair, I wasn't thinking clearly.

Still, I could have sworn I didn't see that bike.

"What's wrong with your face?" Libby asks. "You look . . . ugly."

I sigh. "Thanks, Libby. I'm thinking."

"Also, gross, is that jelly?" She crouches to better examine the scattered donuts. "Strawberry?"

I stoop to pick them up. I'll toss them in the trash in the kitchen. Hopefully Davey's parents won't wonder about them. I wonder if sex donuts were a thing when they were my age? "Mr. and Mrs. Fried?" I yell. "Are you home yet? We just came by to feed the dogs."

I wait a second but nobody answers.

My phone buzzes again and I groan when I see who it is.

Text from 262-352-3553 (mobile):
Hey gurl, u feelin crazy? Sad? Doc dan's got potions 2 cure u, it's my dick, call me baby XXX DOLLAR DAN XXX

This is the fifth text I've gotten from him today. He keeps asking if he and I can get together now that my boyfriend's "halfway out the door." (I'd like to strangle him.)

"What's wrong?" Libby asks, seeing my face.

"Nothing," I lie, checking the time. It's eleven. "We should leave in about twenty minutes," I tell her. "Miss Rosa's bringing home lunch."

"Yummy," she says, apparently expecting to be included in said lunch.

I glance at her. "Don't you have to carve Jesus for the Frostbite Challenge?"

"Meh. I'm bored of it. Besides, I know we're gonna win."

"You can split whatever she brings me, if you want."

"Cool." She starts pulling off her boots. "Gah, I can't believe Davey was alone here so much. Big house for one person." She yanks her head away as Pasta tries to slobber on her face.

I nod. "You want to hear something crazy about that, actually?"

"Duh," Libby says, pursing shut her mouth to avoid accidentally French kissing the dog.

"One time Davey was like, 'Hey, Mom and Dad, I get that you're totally upset about your kid dying—she was my sister, I'm upset, too—but, like, maybe you could stay home more because *I'm still alive*.' And they said, 'We're not alive, honey.'"

"Creepy," Libby says softly.

I nod. "Let's search the living room."

"You go ahead. I'll start upstairs," she says, reaching for her purse.

"Good idea. Cover more ground."

The living room is exactly how the EMTs left it. The

coffee table is shattered and there are aspirin bottles everywhere. Sheriff Staake should have taken these in for fingerprints. Though I guess if they were the family's stash of aspirin, then everybody's touched them.

"Hey, come look at this!" Libby yells.

Pasta Batman yaps sharply from the foyer.

"Lemme deal with the dogs real quick." I call them both into the kitchen, then crank open the back door so they can do their business while I pour some kibble in their bowls.

But instead of pooping in the snow, both dogs turn on their heels and run back in, barking like crazy. "What the fuck, Marco."

I turn around to see a masked man blocking the back doorway, and drop the kibble, screaming.

"Whoa, whoa, whoa," he says, yanking at his camouflage mask.

Libby pounds down the stairs and careens into the room, skidding on her socks. "What?" she screams. "What in the name of—oh, hi Sheriff Staake."

"I told the Frieds I'd feed their animals," Staake says, folding his balaclava in his hands. "Also, I left my gun here last night." He slides the door shut behind him.

"Why were you wearing that?" I ask, gasping for breath.

"What, this?" He holds up the balaclava. "It's cold, Bushman—plus they're on triple sale at the Buck Fleet and trendy to boot. Anyhoo, sorry that I frightened you." He smiles. "Looks like you took care of the dogs so I'll just . . ." He reaches for the kitchen counter and slides a holster belt toward him. I hadn't noticed it before.

"Was that loaded?" I ask.

"Of course it was," he says. "I'm not stupid. I gotta stay ready for anything."

"You left a loaded gun here?" Libby asks, scowling at him. "Just, like, lying around? Why did you even take it off?"

"How did you even have time to take it off?" I add, jumping in. "We weren't here for that long, as far as I can remember."

"Are you two looking to get arrested?" he barks.

We shake our heads. "No, sir."

"The belt's a bit too tight on me, if you want to know the truth," he says quietly. "It gets a wee bit pinchy. Now stay out of trouble, you hear? Because I'm watching you. Buh-bye now." He yanks open the door and tromps back into the snow.

"That was insane," I blurt out once he's gone. "He didn't even ask what we were doing here. Do you think he's following us? Do you think he's the . . . Oh my God, Libby, what if it's him?"

"Also, what kind of sheriff leaves his gun places and then breaks in to get it back? I mean, Gah," she says. "My grandma has a drinking problem, too, but you don't see her leaving her rifles around willy-nilly then just prancing onto private property to find them. She has a gun safe like every other sane person. Anyway, come on, there's that thing I gotta show you."

"But wait—"

"No, I don't think Sheriff Staake plotted your boyfriend's supposed suicide attempt," she says, waving me along. "For one thing, do you really think he'd be able to plan that sort of thing? He's too drunk to function, for Gah's sake."

"That's true, I guess."

As we pass through the living room, Libby snatches a liter of vodka from under the bar. "Can I take this?" She holds up the bottle.

"Um."

"I'm taking it. Davey's sober anyway. Now follow me, you've got to see his bedroom. It's not evidence exactly, but anyone who says he wanted to die last night is a total idiot, for sure, because it's just . . . Well, come on."

I follow her upstairs. She pushes open his bedroom door.

"See?" she asks. "You wanted romance last night, remember? And he went for it."

White rose petals are scattered all across the bed, and candles are covering every square inch of desk, dresser, and end table. "Look how excited he was," Libby says. I watch her pick up one of the candles and sniff it, and feel a pang where my heart should be. None of this was here last night. I think I made Sheriff Staake look everywhere with me. My thoughts feel sped up. "Vanilla. That's intense. That means he really thought about it—hey, are you okay?"

"Someone was here after we left last night," I mumble. "Whoever did this, they . . ." I try to focus on the rose petals, but they're moving, fluttering on Davey's freshly made bed—as if there's a breeze coming through the stuffy room. "They came back to mess with my head."

"Kippy?" Libby shouts. "Wait, I'm sorry, I thought you'd be happy," she is saying. The words are faraway and heavy, like we're underwater. Her face is a throbbing, telescopic pinpoint. The floor beneath my feet is quicksand.

"Oh my Gah!" Libby says, plunking down beside me on Miss Rosa's couch. "I know you said you don't want to talk about it or whatever, but I can't stop thinking about your face when you fainted, just like, 'UGGGHHHH'"—she reaches in front of her, clawing the air, mimicking my fall—"no offense. Do you have diabetes or something? Since when do you faint? Wait. Tell me the truth"—she blinks at me—"are you dying of cancer? In movies when people faint they're dying of cancer. Or else they're pregnant. Oh my Gah you're pregnant."

"You have to have sex to get pregnant," I say, tapping my pencil against the list of evidence I've compiled so far.

1. Shadow man
2. Ralph voice mail
3. No blood alcohol
4. Bedroom display
5. Ralph is insane and capable of anything

"Is it narcolepsy?" Her eyes get wide. "Oh my Gah, is it aliens?"

Part of me wants to tell her everything: the nightmares, the fainting spells, how the shadowy figure at Davey's house looked a lot like one of my hallucinations. The other part of me needs her on my side and knows that if she finds out how real my flashbacks can be, she'll probably turn into everyone else, and start questioning what we're up to. She'll stop helping me.

"No, it's never happened before," I lie. "I was just . . . just thinking about someone sneaking back into Davey's house."

She looks bored.

"Also, I don't know." I shrug. "Being in Davey's bedroom. You know what I mean?"

"Ohhhh," Libby says knowingly. "So it was like a princess fainting sort of thing."

"What?"

"You know," she says, flapping her hands. "Like, they're standing there with their humongous ponytails, and their animal friends, and the prince shows up, but they thought he was dead, and it's all too much, and then: KABOOM!"

I don't know what she's talking about, but I nod. The annoying truth about my fainting spells is that they're pretty unpredictable. Plus, I definitely didn't feel like much of a delicate princess up in Davey's bedroom—more like a selfish sex fiend who couldn't stop thinking, *If only I hadn't let Libby talk my ear off in the car—and put my hair up in a bun and reassure me and, like, generally be a friend and stuff—I would have gotten here in time, fought off the bad guy, and Davey would have been like, "Whoa, you saved me," and I would have been like, "Yeah, that's cuz I'm a hero. Now let's get boned." Then I would have led him to the perfect bedroom with the perfect roses. And it would have been perfect, and my negligee would have matched the décor, like in some kind of good dream, and I wouldn't be sitting here drenched in sweat next to the hottest girl in school trying to find out who ruined everything before they kill me first.*

"Sorry," I mutter, seeing the look on Libby's face. "I went to a place."

"What's with all these knives lying on the carpet, anyway?"

"Just be glad I disarmed the booby traps."

The back door slams and I hear Miss Rosa kicking off her snow boots in the kitchen. At the sight of Libby and me sprawled out on her couch, she harrumphs, clutching a greasy bag of fast food protectively to her chest. "Who is new girl?" she asks. The smells of hot hamburgers and dirty snow fill the living room. "Rosa has two meats, for two peoples. Three? Too many." I stuff the list back into my backpack, along with a bunch of crumpled doctor's notes and half-finished letters to Ralph.

"That's okay," Libby says, smiling. "Kippy said she'd share with me."

Miss Rosa nods approvingly. "Soup is on," she says, unpacking the bag.

"Sorry for inviting someone over without asking you," I say. "It's just you said to feel at home, so . . ."

"Is not problem," she says. "So long as Rosa gets whole

hamburger, is okay."

"Cool, yeah, we just went for a quick drive, or whatever, so—"

"You leave house?" she shouts, immediately enraged. "There is strange man with rope of evil and you go around by selves?"

"Wait, what?" I shake my head. "What's a rope of evil?"

"Oh." She scowls. "Is other thing. Bad memory from Rosa's brain. Anyway," she continues, smiling, "I call police but they say, 'No understand you, foreigner, go back to Russia.' American monsters! Russia!" She spits. "Is Poland. Even Dom, he is too angered about Davey and 'statutory rape' to believe this danger. Everyone is missing, how do you say, the dagger?"

"The . . . point?"

"Yes, everyone missing point. Is disgusting." She crosses the room and pats my head and shoulders. "But you are okay? No missing limbs, is good. What happens? What do you see? When you go outside, you bring knives, yes? Please tell Rosa you bring with you at least one knife." She frowns. "I give you so many nice knives," she says, gesturing to the weapons scattered on the floor. "And you leave them here, don't you?"

"Sorry," I mumble.

Rosa shakes her head, her wide eyes magnified by her thick glasses. "Soup is on and the police, they hide like pathetic *wilk*—how do you say, *wilk*?" She growls and bares her teeth, moving her tiny fingers through the air like a claw.

"Wolf?"

She presses a hand to her forehead, angry at herself for forgetting. "Yes, of course. Wolf. Baby creature. Is sad like peanut. In Poland, we feel so unhappy for wolf."

Libby shakes her head. "Wolves are considered scaredy-cats in Poland? Here they're just . . . scary."

"Poles fear nothing except for Beelzebub. He is demons. The *wilk*, eh. They run and howl in the dark, like wretched babies. Good only for meats." She hands me a hamburger wrapped in paper. "Eat."

"Thank you."

"Yeah, thanks," Libby says, picking at my french fries.

"I want you to be safe," Rosa says, cramming hand-fuls of onion rings into her mouth. "You"—she points to Libby—"with the *pierski kobiece*, the bing bongs size of small moons. You know man, he is monster for *kobiece*. You must attack to survive. And you"—she nods at me, still scarfing down her 'meats'—"baby tiger, you have claws and teeths but you are too small." She sighs softly. "My *zabko*, my *robaczku*, you have the bird bones. Your *koteczek* face is 'talk to me please' face, you are my heart and my moon, but you are mouse—"

"Miss Rosa," I mutter, feeling my face turn red. Her endearments can get a little over the top.

"Miss Rosa learn you self-defense," she says decisively, swallowing another huge chunk of hamburger. "After meats, we go, is field trip." The next bite is so big that I think she's going to choke.

"Do you know the Heimlich?" I whisper to Libby.

"Ew," she says, "the what?"

But after a few minutes of determined gulping, it's a moot point: The goiter-like lump in Miss Rosa's neck is gone and she flashes us a smile full of ground beef. "Soup is on, my chickens," she says, her voice all hoarse. "Today I am teaching you the murder."

"Message sent today, December 22, at 11:00 a.m.:

'Hi, Kippy, it's um . . . Well, it's Jim Steele again.
I know we don't usually talk but uh . . . look, I just
wanted to tell you that, between you and me . . .

'Well, Kippy, my college roommate committed
suicide when I was at Princeton and . . . it's not
something that I usually talk about, but he and I were
close and . . .

'I guess I'm just reiterating the fact that if you'd
like to talk about it . . .

'Well, I'm here. It's lonely sometimes, but you
don't have to be alone.'

"End of message. To delete this message press seven, to
save it press nine—

"BEEEEEEEEP.

"Message deleted."

WE THREE KINGS

"Is only for very, very bad times," Miss Rosa says sternly, offering me a knife handle first. Rosa's been trying to teach me self-defense techniques ever since she got together with my dad, but this is the first time I've let her bring me to Knock Em Bop Em, Friendship's shooting range, where they keep the sawdust dummies and extra targets.

Technically it's a storage closet, but it looks more like the sort of place a serial killer goes to be alone or have tea parties with his corpses. Someone's lined the dummies against one wall, facing us, and there's a long aisle cleared, and duct tape on the linoleum where you're supposed to stand when you chuck the knives at their faces. Apparently Miss Rosa once taught anger-management stuff to the owners, free of charge, so now they're letting us practice back here as a favor.

"Decorate this face with knife," Rosa says, pointing at the dummy. "Pretend is Rolph."

She calls Ralph Rolph. One time in the hospital, I awoke to her standing over me muttering some kind of "kill Rolph" mantra chant thing. When she saw that I was awake, she said, "Kippy, give hand. I teaching you how to make fist for to punch the Rolph." At the time I was too sleepy from the drugs in my system to even squeeze, but she made me go through the basic motions of shoving my palm upward at her nose, which she said was the most efficient way to kill a man in one fluid motion. "Bone goes into brain," she said, "he die, you learn." She's very protective of me, when it comes down to it, which is a nice sentiment, I guess. Especially since she's not trying to be my mom or anything, regardless of what Dom says. (I cannot imagine my mom handing me a giant switchblade before bed and saying, "Good night, *robaczku*.")

"Oh my Gah, look at this," Libby says, laughing. She's in the corner behind us, pawing through the storage trays marked *Hostage Targets*. She's totally ignored everything Miss Rosa's said so far, and hasn't even looked at all the knives Miss Rosa laid out on the nearby folding table—which I feel bad about since Miss Rosa is obviously proud of them.

"And remember me, Kippy: murdering only for emergencies," Miss Rosa says, emphasizing each word.

"What counts as an emergency?" Libby asks, suddenly alert.

Miss Rosa grunts, putting her hands on my hips to adjust my stance. "Maybe you are rape, maybe you are murder, maybe you are might be."

"Maybe I am murder," I repeat, wishing Davey were here to laugh at all this.

"Have you ever stabbed someone?" I ask Rosa.

She snorts.

"Have you?" I ask, raising my eyebrows.

She sighs. "Once, I have girlfriend—"

"Girlfriend," Libby snaps. "Like a lesbian?"

Rosa shushes her. "Isadora, she has son, and he eats part of my arm."

"He *bit* you?"

"No, full eat. Bites and swallows. I get tattoo of flowers for to cover." She rolls up her sleeve and shows me the flower. It's really badly drawn and dips in where a chunk of her arm is missing.

"So you stabbed him?"

"A little, but I drop knife, and he eats more of my arm."

Libby makes a gagging noise.

"So did you dump her after that?" I ask.

"Dump?" Rosa narrows her eyes at me. "Is this the poop word?"

"No, like break up," I explain. "Your girlfriend. Isadora. After her son ate more of your arm . . . I don't know. . . . Was the romance over?"

"Oh." She sighs. "Isadora is saying . . . how do you say, bad power?"

I think for a sec. "Evil?"

"No."

"Bad *influence*," Libby says, nodding knowingly. "Everybody thinks I'm a bad influence."

Rosa grunts. "This is word. Bad influence. She take Adolf and they go countryside to live in forest like animals."

"No way," I say. "Her kid ate your arm and she blamed *you*?"

"You only stabbed him in self-defense," Libby says, examining her nails.

"Ehhh." Rosa grits her teeth, looking guilty. "One thing I do not tell before is . . . I bite Adolf first. Only one ear now, he is having."

It's quiet for a long time.

"So you're, like, a real lesbian then," Libby says finally.

Rosa shrugs. "I am not knowing."

"Oh." Libby flips her hair over one shoulder. "Well, Kippy's probably better at definitions, but being a lesbian is, like, when—"

"I know what is lesbian," Rosa says. "I love Isadora once, and now I love Dommy. Is fine." She squints at me. "Actually sometimes I am thinking your father is lesbian."

"I don't know how to respond to that," I grumble.

"She's kind of right." Libby says. "Your dad is, like, almost identical to Rosie O'Donnell—physically, I mean. Personality-wise he's more like . . . I don't know. Maybe the teapot in *Beauty and the Beast*? *Hey*, look at this." She yanks a huge sheet of paper off the top of the target pile. On it, Sheriff Staake's face is laced with target lines. He's pointing a gun. "I cannot *wait* to post this on Facebook. I want to hang it in my room. He's so *fat*." She cocks her head. "I just . . . What does he eat?"

I smile. This is fun. Just a few gals having gal time at a shooting range with knives.

But then I frown. "Guys, do you think our friendship passes the Bechdel test?"

"Uggggggh," Libby says, sounding so bored. "*Bechdel* is the stupidest word I've ever heard, and I hate quizzes."

"What is this Bechdel?" Rosa asks. "Is doctor?"

I take a deep breath. "No, it's like . . . it's like this test for whether a female relationship is meaningful. Like, if they ever talk about anything other than guys, it's a real, meaningful relationship, and it passes the Bechdel test. But if not . . . Well, then you're kind of just like this victim to cultural norms and societal pressures—"

"Is stupid," Miss Rosa says, nodding.

"I agree with her," Libby mumbles, making a face.

"But critical theory is a really good way of examining our values and untangling knee-jerk prejudice," I insist. Then of course Rosa wants to know what theory is, which is totally hard to translate, but I try my best.

She remains unimpressed. "Theory is sounding to me like fear," she says, nodding at the knife in my hand. "Now throw. I am not wanting for you to bleed fingers. But when you throw, throw by blades. Goes smoother."

I stare at the dummies lined up against the wall,

"Throw," she screams.

I toss the first knife and it lands halfway to the targets, hitting the concrete floor with a feeble *twang*. "Shit," I mutter.

Libby laughs. "Again," she cheers, clapping her hands. "Again!"

"Is okay." Miss Rosa hands me another knife. "We will

take many times practice." She hooks her thumbs through the belt loops on her elastic pants. "But when you hit target, I will give knives for you to keep. Also candies." She shimmies, and I recognize the distinctive sound of loose M&M'S clacking in her pockets. She used to keep M&M'S in her pockets to motivate those of us in her anger management group. I guess she never noticed that none of us ever wanted them, since they had been removed from their packaging and were rolling around in lint, adhering to one another from her groin sweat. "You are liking candies, no? Many prizes for you if you win." She continues shimmying. "Now hit dummy, Kippy. You can do it. Pretend is having Rolph Johnston's evil face."

I envision Ralph charging toward me with his machete, and fling the second knife so hard it bounces off the whitewash brick above the dummies' heads.

Rosa puts a little hand on my arm, gurgling slightly like a pigeon. "You are not focus!"

I want to tell her about the sound of Ralph's voice in my ear, how I want to hurt him badly for what I know he did, but how part of me also wants him to live forever. Hate and love are both obsessions. You can't hate someone without caring, too.

But before I can answer I see a blur in my peripheral vision and hear a soft *hmpph, hmpph, hmpph* across the room, like a basketball swishing cleanly through the hoop, three times. One dummy from the lineup now has three knives protruding from its crotch.

I gape at Libby.

"What?" she asks, all defensive. "My mom and I play darts. Also just because I know where to throw it doesn't make me a slut."

Miss Rosa starts a slow clap and I join in with gusto. Once Libby realizes we're not weirded out by where she aimed, she curtsies very prettily, just like a little girl.

For the rest of the session, Miss Rosa makes me do this thing called a roundhouse kick, using my good leg to give the kick propulsion. It hurts a little to fling my bad leg up like that, and the thought of actually *kicking* something with it nauseates me; the anticipated pain alone is enough to make me queasy. But she makes me practice it over and over, until I'm sweating bullets and worry I might do it in my sleep, just from muscle memory. She says that if I suck at knives, I might as well have another trick up my sleeve.

"Remember," she says, "maybe you are murder."

From: NitaFried3000@hotwahoo.com
To: Kippyyyyyyyyyyyyyyy@memail.com

Dear Kippy,

Davey's father and I have returned from our grief retreat for obvious reasons (Davey's recent accident). Now that we're back we wanted to touch base with you regarding certain expectations.

As you already know, the visitor's list is family only. This is not to hurt your feelings but rather to cocoon ourselves. We've been dealing with Davey's mental health issues as a family for a while now, and we find a certain comfort in doing so privately. Please understand. Davey had been deteriorating mentally for months prior to this most recent cry for help. You might not have known, but that doesn't change the facts.

The doctors are saying they're not sure what will happen. Obviously, we'll let you know if there are any developments.

All the best,

Davey's mom

From: Kippyyyyyyyyyyyyyy@memail.com

To: NitaFried3000@hotwahoo.com

Dear Mrs. Fried,

I'm disappointed but I understand.

I hope you feel better.

Love,

Kippy

DECK THE HALLS

"But what about our knife bonding?" I ask. "We had such fun girl time, and now you're pulling, like, a dicks-before-chicks sort of thing."

"A what?" Rosa asks. "Mud Dumpling, please. My heart is huge for you, but Dommy is boyfriend. Is causing problems."

I cross my arms, feeling like an angry little kid. When we left Knock Em Bop Em, I figured we'd go back to her place—I was going to tell Dr. Ferguson to meet me there. Instead we're idling in my driveway with the car running. Dom and Miss Rosa are going out for their weekly date night, and she says it's probably a good idea for me to go home. Apparently they came to an agreement.

"And what about how it's dangerous out there?" I go

on, hating the sulkiness in my voice. "I thought that you believed me."

"I do! Is why I teach you self-defense," she says, sighing. "You come anytime, Mud Dumpling, always." Her seat is cranked so far forward that her nose is practically touching the wheel. It's hard to be annoyed at somebody so small. "But is bad, I think, when this silence for Dommy goes too long."

I try to remind her without crying that there's a homicidal whacko prowling Friendship's streets and that it's been less than twenty-four hours since I stormed away from Dom and took refuge at her house. I'm feeling pretty desperate, to be honest—I even tried to convince Libby to have a sleepover but her dad kept texting saying that if she didn't get to the Frostbite Challenge grounds lickety-split to work on their Jesus sculpture he was going to go ballistic and enter the contest as a solo contender.

"My father is *not* going to take the glory of Frostbite away from me," Libby said, clenching her teeth before sprinting into the icy parking lot.

"For one thing, I just got the weirdest email from Davey's mom basically admitting she and Mr. Fried both believe that this was some kind of attempted suicide," I tell Rosa now, "and I sort of want to talk to someone until dawn about my feelings, and also I'm scared of Ralph, and also all the weapons are still at your house—"

"Is why I give you knife," she says, rustling in her purse. "I give also to Libby. I like her. She good heart."

"Um, I don't need a knife. I am the type of person who, if given a knife, will likely stab myself by accident."

"What are you, *wilk*?" she asks.

"A little," I admit. "I like being around weapons, I guess, and around people who could potentially use them—but as of now I do not consider myself to be one of those people." I open the passenger door and nearly eat it on the ice. "I'm not exactly the most graceful person, if you haven't noticed—speaking of which, it's going to be totally awkward with Dom."

She wrestles more forcefully through the contents of her purse and pulls out a giant switchblade. "Ah, here," she says, handing it to me. "Tell Dommy I said is okay and remember the booby traps I learn you. Good-bye, *zabko*, my raisin."

"Please tell Dom that my *psychiatrist* is coming over for a visit," I snap, shivering in the cold. I still don't know how much I'm going to tell Dr. Ferguson about everything that's happened, but I'm glad he's coming over. Talking to him always makes me feel slightly less crazy. "So, like, if Dom comes home and sees me sitting with a *man*, he shouldn't think it's because I'm a *slut*—or a *szmata* or whatever."

"You learn Polish!" she says, laying on the horn. This is how she picks Dom up for dates: by honking until he trudges through the snow, smiling all the while like his face might break.

I hear the front door open and skid across the ice to the garage, punching in the code and ducking through before he can see me. I'm dreading our next interaction. I'm not sure I'm ready for whatever awkward apology he has in store. (*I understand that you have certain . . . urges*, I can imagine him saying. *Desire is natural, but . . .*) And if he's not going to apologize—if him treating me like some kind of monster is in fact our new dynamic—I'm not sure I'm ready for that, either.

The garage door cranks shut behind me. I climb onto the riding mower and watch my breath collect in clouds, turning the knife over and over in my hands, trying to calm down. What if whoever hurt Davey breaks into the house before Dr. Ferguson gets here? What if Dom never goes back to normal? What if Davey never wakes up? What if Libby was weirded out by my sleepover invite and never wants to come over again? (And why should that last one matter?) Why is Davey's mom acting so *formal* toward me? If she really thinks he did this to himself, does she also think it's my fault?

I have a lot of feelings.

After a while I hear the car door slam and tires crunching over packed snow. I wait a few more seconds before slinking past Dom's tool bench and opening the door to the kitchen. The questions in my head won't stop swirling. So I lock all the doors. Then I start setting up the snares that Miss Rosa taught me. She probably didn't think I'd cover the entire first floor with booby traps, but that's what I intend to do.

The phone rings when I'm in the middle of a particularly complex snare that involves rigging dental floss to a fire extinguisher. I'd let it go to voice mail but part of me thinks it might be Libby. Maybe she changed her mind about that sleepover.

I step delicately through the web of traps I've laid, careful to place my walking cast just so, and lift the phone from its cradle.

"Hello? Bushman residence."

"Kippy, it's Jim. Is your dad there?"

I know Dom and Jim are working together on the Cloudy Meadows suit, but it's starting to bug me how these used to be people *I* knew—Rosa, Jim, Ferguson—and now Dom has his own relationships with them and, like, has them over for hamburgers and stuff as if they're *his* friends. It's like being left out of a clique you used to rule. Not that I would know what that feels like, either.

"He's on a date," I mutter.

"I see. So . . . Kippy . . . how are you?"

What an insane question. I hate when you know someone doesn't want to talk to you, and you don't want to talk to them, either, but there you are, talking. I guess it's called being polite. "Very well . . . thank you."

"Did you get my messages about—"

"Yeah, but obviously I take issue with the word *suicide*."

"Ah, yes—"

"He's alive, for starters."

"Shit. I'm terrible. Sorry. Look—"

"Davey didn't try to hurt himself," I press on, feeling my heart start to pound. "Someone else attacked him."

He pauses. "Kippy, that's—"

"Crazy?"

It's quiet. I chew at my nails. "Sorry about your roommate, by the way. I should have said that first."

"Thank you," he says. "This might not be the right thing to say to you—or who knows, it might be exactly right to tell you. Personally I don't think that people need to tiptoe around you. Having been on the receiving end of that kind of delicate treatment, I know how irritating it can be."

Oh no, now we're having a heart-to-heart. "Okay." Is that Albus outside or a bush?

It's a bush.

"Ralph Johnston called me today," Jim says.

My heart rate increases slightly. "Why?"

"Something about a storage unit. Bragging about being rich. It was hard to understand."

I take a deep breath and pull myself up on the counter so I won't accidentally step into a trap. "Right, he mentioned that . . . *Star Wars* collectibles. I remember he used to have this gross Chewbacca head—"

"You *talk* to him?"

"Is that illegal?"

"*What?*"

"Look, you're the one calling to chitchat about the guy."

"Technically I was calling to speak with your father." There's a smile in his voice. "You're quick, you know that?"

"Yes, I do."

"So what's with this storage-unit stuff?" he asks. "He offered me money at one point. I told him no out of a sense of loyalty to you, but if it's interesting enough—"

"You mean if there's money in it, screw loyalty."

"Your words, not mine."

"He says he's got a Chewbacca head."

"Yeah, I've seen it."

"Ralph needs money for a lawyer. He's trying to get anyone he can to auction off his old *Star Wars* collectibles. There's hundreds of thousands of dollars' worth of stuff in there."

"Hm."

"I know, right? Too bad you're too devoted to me to help him get any of it."

He's quiet a second. "Is the Chewbacca head the same one worn in the movie?"

"Yeah, totally original. Why?"

He explains that he's been Googling "*Star Wars* collectibles rare" while we've been talking (typical Jim, to half listen when we're discussing tough stuff) and found a weird, anonymous chat room where one guy in Wisconsin is claiming to have the original Chewbacca head for sale.

"The listing's only a few hours old," Jim says. "He's got it listed for two hundred and fifty thousand dollars . . . Jesus, there are already five people interested." He's quiet for a moment, scrolling, I guess. "These idiots might be rich but they cannot spell. You should see these comments."

I take a few deep breaths, trying to stay calm about the

fact that someone's helping Ralph. And whoever's selling the Chewbacca head might be the same guy on the outside who went after Davey.

"Kippy, you there?" Jim asks.

"Maybe we could get some money out of this," I respond, trying to sound casual. Jim's better situated than I am to intimidate Ralph's peddler—with legal recourse, or whatever—and odds are I can probably get him to find out who's helping Ralph if I offer him a boatload of money.

He doesn't say anything.

"Maybe we could get *all* the money out of it," I add. "Then he wouldn't have any cash left over to get some big shot to lie for him at trial. He'll be sure to get what he deserves. And you and I could split the two hundred and fifty thousand dollars."

"And what's this for again, exactly? So you can get back at Ralph for 'causing' your boyfriend's suicidal inklings? You're in denial, you know that?"

I look down at my legs swinging from the counter, focusing on the walking cast. Jim is one of those people who believes in tough love, which I've never understood. Being on the receiving end of bluntness doesn't feel good and it isn't enlightening, either. It only makes me defensive. So what if I want Ralph to call me so badly I feel sick, and at the same time I can't wait to go testify against him at trial so I can cry in front of the jury and get him sent to the electric chair? It's a complicated relationship. I look around at the traps I built and feel infinitely calmer. The weird thing about post-traumatic stress is how you can go from a huge and frightening adrenaline rush—this heart-pounding flight response—to feeling like nothing is real, and you're watching the world spin from a cloud.

"Two hundred and fifty thousand dollars," I respond finally, drawing out each syllable.

"You're freaking me out, kid," Jim says. But I know he's thinking about the money, and I can picture his face spreading into that evil grin he has whenever he stands a chance of making bank. "But, I don't know. . . . This might be fun. Hell, it'd give you a distraction, right? Hundreds of thousands of dollars."

"Totally," I say, egging him on. Who cares if he has to tell himself he's being greedy on my behalf? In a way, he is, because he's doing my bidding without even really knowing it.

"I could feign interest in this piece-of-shit geek gear," he continues, "and find out who's selling for Ralph, and spout legalese in their direction until they shit themselves. Then you and I could split . . . Well, let's call it an eighty-five/fifteen break. You get a finder's fee, but I'm doing the grunt work."

"Fine, that's fair. Just one thing."

"Yeah?"

"I want to know who's selling it."

He makes an exasperated noise.

"I don't care if you think I'm delusional," I continue. "I wanna know who's selling Ralph's stuff. It's the least you can do since I'm sending you in the direction of, like, two new vacation homes, or whatever the hell you spend your money on."

A car rumbles up the driveway.

"Okay?" I demand. "I want you to see this guy in person."

"Deal, kid," he says. "But don't tell your dad—he'd kill me for playing along with . . . with whatever this is."

The idea that he and Dom have ever discussed my mental health makes me wobbly and furious.

"I've got to go to therapy now," I tell him, watching through the window as Dr. Ferguson slams his car door.

"Tell Ferguson I owe him a phone call about this lawsuit," Jim says. "You're lucky to have him, you know. He's taking big swings for you. But will you remind him he has paperwork I need?"

"Yeah, sure. Keep me posted about the Chewbacca head."

"Promise me you won't go causing trouble."

The doorbell rings.

I replace the phone in its cradle and skulk carefully to the front door—disarming the cast iron skillet I've rigged there in order to let in Dr. Ferguson.

"So," he says, spotting the mess of traps behind me. "Should we start by talking about whatever all that is?"

"No, thanks," I mumble, and lead him somewhere safe. "We'll sit in my bedroom."

"I need to talk to you about something, Kippy," he says, following me up the stairs.

"Yeah?" I say, running my hand up the bannister as we pass Bushman family classics framed against the wall: Mom and Dom on their wedding day, his mustache and her thick blond hair, that dress with poofy sleeves; the three of us sitting on the lawn; Dom and I alone at my eleventh birthday party, the first one after she died. "It's this way," I say, cutting off Ferguson as he starts to talk again and leading him down another dark hallway to my pink-and-white bedroom. I gesture at the pink desk chair for him to sit and plop down on the springy bed. I wish Dom would let me redecorate. "What is it?" I ask.

"I understand that Ralph Johnston has been phoning you—the Green Bay Correctional Facility has informed me," he says carefully, readjusting his weight in the little chair. "An officer overheard him on the pay phone and thought that I should know."

I sigh. First Sheriff Staake calls Dr. Ferguson, then Ralph's frigging prison. You'd think he was my animal handler, or something.

"Like you, Ralph is also one of my patients."

"What?" My voice is surprisingly quiet, but my mouth is open so wide that I can feel my tongue drying up. "What. The. Fu—"

"Wait," he says, holding up a hand before I can fully respond to this bomb he's dropped. "I started treating him before you and I began working together. The correctional facilities often call me to work with inmates. Up until very recently, as you know, I was a psychiatrist for a state-run sanatorium, so it's only natural—"

"But you're helping me prepare to testify against him," I sputter. "What are you, like, a double agent? Isn't this illegal? Does he get to hear about me, too?"

"Of course not—please just let me finish." He licks his lips, looking pained. "I didn't have to tell you this, Kippy—I shouldn't be telling it to you. But I think that you're wise enough to—"

"I'm sick of all these men in my life telling me how smart I am like it's some sort of prize," I snap. "As if I didn't already know, when really you are the ones who are only just now picking up on it."

"Okay," he says carefully, like I might bite. "May I finish? There's nothing wrong with working with Ralph and you simultaneously. What's unethical is actually the fact that I'm mining my sessions with him for information about how to put him away for as long as possible."

"But—"

The ringing in my ears abates a little. So this is what Jim Steele meant about Dr. Ferguson taking big swings on our behalf. "But why?" I ask. "What's in it for you?" Dr. Ferguson already left Cloudy Meadows. Now he relies on private-practice-type jobs. If anyone in a position to do something about it finds out that he's compromising his confidentiality clause with Ralph to help *me*, he could get disbarred, or whatever the medical equivalent is. He'd never be able to get a client ever again.

He examines his hands. "I'm a doctor and I believe in science. But I also believe in God." He glances at me warily.

I think of Libby, and her moments of weird grace. Like how she'll make a face about my hair, but then drop everything to help me on behalf of some higher power. Faith is inherently irrational, but it's also one of the only ways to have really firm principles. It's often a marker of kindness, too.

"I could have handled it," I say, "knowing about Ralph being your patient and everything—and personally I think that acting like I can't handle the truth is just another way of saying that I'm batshit crazy and unstable, which is honestly offensive." Still, it's true that he didn't have to tell me. I never would have found out. If Ralph was going to tell me, he would have done so right away instead of writing to me about *Chad*, or whatever fake name he fed me.

"We didn't want you to have to lie—on the off chance that the defense asked you about it, we wanted you to be able to answer truthfully."

"You mean Dom and Jim Steele knew about this?" I mumble. "You guys treat me like a little kid."

"There are people whom you see on a semiregular basis who are also my patients," he says, sounding defensive now. "The number isn't incredibly high, but you'd be surprised."

"So now you're coming clean about Ralph so that you can lecture me about accepting his calls."

"*No.* It's so that I can reassure you that I've lectured him about making such calls. Ralph is not supposed to get in touch with you, and the fact that he did has landed him in lots of trouble. I am so sorry for that, Kippy. He's just trying to manipulate you. It's classic sociopathy."

I play with the coverlet on my bed. It's too frilly. "Does he ask about me?"

"Kippy—"

"I just want to know what he says."

Dr. Ferguson laces his fingers over one knee. "Let's talk about the fact that he called you, and how he made you feel. Tell me more about that."

"I feel nothing."

"What did we decide about triggers?"

"To avoid them, but—"

"Ralph Johnston gets energy from controlling people," Dr. Ferguson says, starting to sound impatient. "If you let him hear even a smidge of reluctance or pain or complexity or rage in your voice it will make him indescribably happy. Do you understand? Is that what you want? For him to reach nirvana in there?"

"No."

He nods, apparently satisfied. "Was his phone call today the extent of your interaction with him?"

I think about the letter in the desk drawer ten inches from where Dr. Ferguson is sitting.

"I've been thinking a lot about Albus," I say, trying to change the subject.

"Adele Botkins?" he asks, smiling.

"She calls herself Albus," I say defensively. "I believe in calling people what they want to be called."

"Are you still having the hallucinations?"

"Sometimes," I admit.

"Remember what I said: It's normal to think you see the people you miss most—it's because you want to see them so badly."

"Right. Seeing things that aren't there is totally normal." I roll my eyes.

"This is hard enough as it is without you being hard on yourself, too," he says gently. "Have you been trying those affirmations we talked about?" He wants me to put Post-its on my mirror that say, *You are beautiful. You are enough.* He wants me to tell myself every day that I am powerful.

"They're too embarrassing." As far as I'm concerned, the only thing more pathetic than seeing things that aren't there, having nightmares that occasionally make me cry like a baby, and sweating through my clothes every time I think I smell blood, would be sauntering around talking to myself, saying shit like, *I'm Kippy Fucking Bushman.*

"Okay." He nods. "Do you want to talk about Adele— sorry, Albus?"

I smile a little. "Kinda."

He leans back in the pink desk chair, smiling. "Personally I thought she was incredible. *She* thought she was a British police officer. That was the only problem." He laughs. "She helped you escape, if I'm not mistaken. She was secretly my favorite patient."

"Mine, too." I can't believe it's taken me so long to follow up about her. "You're already breaking so many rules. It probably wouldn't hurt for you to tell me about her—or at least, like, how she was doing the last time you saw her, before you retired from Cloudy Meadows."

"She actually went home."

"Oh, cool!"

"Very cool."

"Why didn't you tell me that?"

"Didn't I?" He looks surprised. "Her family moved to England—well, back. They lived there for a period, hence her fascination with Scotland Yard."

"That's so great." I force a smile, wondering why she didn't call me when she got out. "That's great for her."

"Are you ready to talk about Davey now?" Dr. Ferguson asks gently.

I shake my head. "Not to someone who doesn't believe me."

"You're still sure he didn't hurt himself?"

"Yes."

"How are things with your father?"

I tell him about Dom's blowup after I came home from the hospital and about spending the night at Miss Rosa's. I leave out the part about the knife throwing. If I've learned anything about well-intentioned adults, it's that no matter how much you trust them, you still can't spill your guts entirely.

"He called me a *szmata*. Or . . . that was Miss Rosa's translation. It means slut."

"That's very hurtful."

"At first he thought Davey had pressured me and when he found out that I hadn't gotten raped, he was mad."

"How upsetting."

"I know. Especially because it's like . . . I didn't even get to . . . you know. So now I'm paying for this crime I didn't even commit—not that having sex is even a crime to begin with." I rake my fingers through my hair and glance at him. "So? Go ahead, do what you do, analyze it."

"You're right when you say you've done nothing wrong. Your father is overreacting to certain inevitable changes—"

"Oof, please don't call them changes. It reminds me of puberty."

"What's wrong with that?"

"Are you kidding? It was the worst. When I got my period, Dom never talked to me about it. All he did was leave all these books out, and he was totally frazzled. I ended up getting so embarrassed that I went and sat in the empty tub with all my clothes on—including, you know, the stained polka-dot stretch pants—and then Dom came in wearing dishwashing gloves, being like, 'What do you need me to do?' Like it was a joke or something.

"It really freaked me out, him standing there with those gloves, like some kind of . . . fake doctor. I ended up slamming the door in his face and staying in there for hours trying to flush my pants down the toilet until the whole thing overflowed—which, I mean, obviously I was old enough to know that would cause problems with the plumbing." I take a deep breath. "I just didn't want him involved anymore. He's always so involved."

"Thank you for sharing it with me." Dr. Ferguson leans back. "Kippy, in what ways do you think his overinvolvement has affected your behavior?"

"Well, it's just that . . . I guess after that I dealt with everything myself." I shrug. "I mean, with certain things. He still takes care of me. But I don't even like the idea of him changing the wastebaskets in my bathroom. I wrap up all my tampons in tissues, put them in my pockets, and throw them out in the bathroom at school."

My phone buzzes.

Text from 262-352-3553 (mobile):
honey u sexi how about u cmere ur bf's sleeping he
don't currrrr XXX DOLLAR DAN XXX

I make a face. Is Dollar Dan's text something I talk about in therapy now or should I wait ten years?

"So you sublimate your sexuality in order to appease your father," Ferguson is saying. Seems like we have a lot to discuss before we get to sexual harassment.

"I don't like *father* and *sexuality* in the same sentence," I say, turning off my phone.

"*Sublimate . . . appease . . .*" He flicks his wrist. "Fancy words that simply mean you've gone out of your way to protect him. You've guarded him from everything, and now he realizes how much you've grown up. I'm not defending him, just trying to emphasize the shock he must have felt once the blinders came off."

"Yeah. But he's still being a weirdo."

"Occasionally a father may behave strangely when he senses his daughter is becoming sexual. In certain cases, he may temporarily rescind his love in an effort to reinfantilize her—to bring her crawling back to him as the child he once knew."

"I guess," I say. "He just needs to get off my nuts. He stresses me out." The words untighten my chest a bit. This seems to be the gist of weekly therapy: I sort of squirm but then I always leave feeling a little lighter.

"You could tell him that," Dr. Ferguson says quietly. "I think it would be entirely fair for you to say that to him."

I hear Rosa's car crunch on the snowy driveway outside. It's already been an hour or so since they left. The minutes with Ferguson fly by. Maybe I will say it to Dom—just, you know, *I'd love it if you could react less strongly to the stuff I'm going through, because it's my life, and it's hard enough going through it myself without dealing with your feelings on top of everything else.*

The back door slams and I hear the fire extinguisher farting endless white foam.

"Kippy," Dom calls, and the way he says it fills the whole house even though he isn't shouting. "What the heck is this contraption? What's this stuff on me? Dr. Ferguson, if you're here I'd like an explanation of my daughter's behavior, please." I hear him curse a little to himself, stomping around.

Another trap goes off and he screams.

Dr. Ferguson bites his lip like he's trying not to laugh. "Sounds like he got caught in a few of your booby traps. We should probably go give him a towel, and then I should probably go."

WHAT CHILD IS THIS?

The next morning Mildred calls and says she needs to chat. In person.

"About what?" I ask warily, thinking of the texts and voice mail messages and Facebook posts I've gotten. Late last night McKetta wrote on my wall, *RIP Davey—he's with the angels, babe,* to which I commented: *HE'S NOT DEAD MCKETTA AND IF HE WERE THIS WOULD STILL NOT BE APPROPRIATE.* Apparently that made her mad because she started a group called "Kippy, Ugh." And now I've lost 120 Facebook friends. Also she may or may not have called the Teen Tip Line on me because Sheriff Staake showed up at our door in the wee hours to see if I was there, safe and sound in my bed, or out huffing paint like somebody said I was.

"I just want to talk," Mildred says.

"If it's about my boyfriend, I'd rather not talk about it," I tell her, trying to sound polite. "I'm sick of people telling me how sorry they are about his so-called suicide attempt—"

"That's what I want to talk to you about," she says. "I think something else happened. And I have proof—come over when you can."

I immediately hang up, grab the list I started making, and phone Libby, who agrees to give me a ride.

From where we're sitting in Mildred's sunroom, you can see Davey's whole house.

"Here we go, an entire wall of my biggest gingerbread architecture, cut into portions," Mildred says, placing a tray of crumbled cookie on the coffee table. "So glad you ladies stopped by. I don't usually have guests, so it's either this or venison, which I would need to defrost." She chuckles loudly. "You can't exactly fit a full leg in the microwave, if you know what I mean!"

"Oh, you really didn't have to demolish a whole gingerbread house for us," I tell her, politely scooping up a handful and shoveling it into my mouth. I motion for Libby to do the same but she shakes her head at me. Some crumbs fall onto my lap and two cats immediately jump up onto my thighs to eat the scraps.

Mildred shoos them off. "Off Dancer, off Prancer! I change their names depending on the holiday. Last Easter they were Jesus and the Bunny."

She plops down between us on the couch and reaches over Libby to turn on the space heater. "Pretty nippy in here with all the windows, but I like the sunshine. Keeps me sane. Otherwise I get a little kooky. Vitamin D cures the crazy, I've read."

Libby finally chimes in. "Oh my Gah, yeah, so welcoming."

"So what's up, Mildred?" I ask her.

"I know I don't . . . come off so great," she says. "I see how people look at me. But I just thought—well, it made sense, see, I thought, *Enough has happened to that boy*—and . . . Well, I kept thinking maybe if I kept an eye on him, I could help. I could protect him." She flops her hands helplessly. "Ever since Marion left to be an alligator farmer I've been a mess, to tell the truth."

I glance at Libby. "Marion's her ex-boyfriend," I explain. "We were all in Rosa's Non-Violent Communication Group together. Before she was my bus driver."

"I didn't want to say anything at first because, you know, I mind my own beeswax. I might be a little off-kilter, I'm the first to admit it, but I keep my trap shut, which isn't easy around here. Folks were gossiping about my Davey everywhere yesterday—the grocery store, the liquor store, the bowling alley, saying that he swallowed all those pills." She wipes her eyes and then pats my thigh. "Nice legs, by the way. We're going to miss you on the bus."

"Mildred," I say gently, removing her heavy, calloused hand from my knee. "You said you wanted to talk about Davey. You said you had proof that—"

"I've got the video if you want to see it," she says. "I'll show it to you if you promise not to get me in trouble. I really don't want to go back to Cloudy Meadows."

"I know," I tell her, putting her hand back on my knee.

"I saw a car drive up," Mildred says. "And there were people running out of the house, if I was seeing correctly—though I'm the first to admit I see things funny sometimes. Bad eyes, for starters. And they did a bunch of shock therapy when I was at Cloudy Meadows, so sometimes my brain feels dumb."

She pops the VHS tape into her old-fashioned VCR, and starts to fast-forward. The first two hours are just of her in her underwear, painstakingly building the gingerbread house.

"You filmed yourself building a gingerbread house?" Libby asks.

"So?" Mildred roars. She presses Play. "Here's where I decided to add button candies for the windows, see? Isn't that great?"

Libby and I nod in unison, mumbling a patchwork of lies: "Great"—"Really exciting stuff"—"Like watching an action movie."

Satisfied, she speeds ahead through more gingerbread-house building. "There," she says at last, pushing Play on the video to reveal a triumphant-looking Mildred along-side one of the largest gingerbread mansions I have ever seen. It basically looks like a giant mound of frosting with little army men on top of it, and Lego trees all along the periphery. "The guesthouse kind of got lost in the artistic process," she says.

In the video, Mildred looks up like she's heard some-thing and approaches the camera. The footage goes sloppy as she drags the camera off the mount and tries to focus it through the window on Davey's house.

Libby and I lean in to see better.

"And there's the car," Mildred says, pointing.

"Where?" Libby asks.

"There." She taps a finger on the dark TV screen, between the leafless skeletons of trees at the edge of her lawn.

"I don't see anything," Libby says. "It looks like a glare or something."

"Me neither," I admit, squinting. "Well, sort of, maybe." Framed between the trees, you can just make out something that kind of looks like a car.

"Watch for headlights," Mildred says.

Sure enough, a pair of lights flash like someone's unlocking the car. A figure running across the lawn is illuminated by the quick burst.

"There he is!" I say.

"I still don't see anything," says Libby.

Mildred rewinds. "Whoever it is, there's someone with 'em."

She pauses the footage and points to what *might* be a figure on-screen.

"I still don't see anything," Libby says, her voice apologetic.

"Right there, see? He bends to grab somebody and scoops 'em up into his arms."

"Have you shown this to anyone?" I ask.

"Of course I ain't shown nobody!" Mildred makes a face. "I figured Davey was having a party or something, and when the cops showed up, I didn't want to get him in trouble. Then I heard what really happened, but I didn't want to change my story."

I pat her arm reassuringly. "They wouldn't have listened to you anyway."

"Listened to her about what?" Libby presses on. "I'm bored of this, you guys. There's nothing here. It's like I'm staring at one of those magic eye posters."

"It's an old model," Mildred says. "It's blurry on the close-ups."

My phone buzzes in my hand. It's Dollar Dan again, asking if I want to hang out. Well, that's being euphemistic: specifically he wants to know if I want to "ride mini Dan like a cowgirl." He repulses me.

"Hey, Mildred," I say, staring at my phone. "How tall would you say the bigger guy was? Maybe five-ten?"

"Maybe," she says uncertainly.

When are you going to get rid of that boyfriend of yours? Or do you want me to get rid of him? "Kind of big? Like a football player?" Dollar Dan was always obsessed with Ralph, too. Maybe obsessed enough to write him some fan mail. And Ralph's smart—he would have been able to identify Dollar Dan as a potential puppet.

1. Shadow man
2. Ralph voice mail
3. No blood alcohol
4. Bedroom display
5. Ralph is insane and capable of anything

6. Ralph is rich enough to pay an accomplice

7. Accomplice: needs to be either totally crazy or desperate enough for money <u>to become crazy</u>

8. <u>Mildred's VHS tape: figures 1 AND 2</u>

Libby rolls her eyes. "What are you getting at, Kippy?"

I tap my list. "Money or no money, Dollar Dan is bat-shit insane."

"What in the glory heck are you talking about?"

"Can you give me one more ride?"

She throws her head back. "Uggghhh."

"Thank you, Libby."

I look again at my phone and text back: Hey, Dollar Dan, what's your address?

The icicles hanging from Dollar Dan's gutters are more than three feet long—as big as the stalactites we learned about in middle school. They're also sharp enough to kill someone. The front porch resembles a throat surrounded by fangs.

"It doesn't even look like anybody lives here," I mutter. The driveway and walkway aren't shoveled. In the middle of the yard, there's a rusted tractor, or something, sticking up through the snow.

"We'll park behind those trees so we can stake it out for a few seconds," Libby says, easing the truck behind some heavy foliage at the end of Dan's lawn.

Just then a screen door bangs shut and we duck down in our seats.

"Is it him?" I ask softly, scrambling for the binoculars Mildred lent us.

Dollar Dan leads a small white terrier toward the end of the unplowed driveway. The snow is so deep that the dog looks like it's swimming in it. Dollar Dan keeps tugging on its leash.

"He's just taking his dog out to pee," I whisper. "Maybe we should get out now and say hi. I like dogs."

"Then he'll know we were spying on him," Libby says, sinking lower in her seat. She yanks the binoculars. "Here, let me see."

"We'll share," I say, giving her one eye.

Dollar Dan pulls the skittering dog farther down the icy driveway to where the trash bins are lined up.

"Good boy, Stewart," he shouts, glancing around as if to see if anyone is watching. Then he yanks Stewart up into the air by the leash and holds him there. The dog spins slowly in circles, its feet twitching off the ground.

Libby grips my arm hard as the dog rotates in midair. It's barely making any noise now.

"Oh my Gah," she says. "I'm not bored of this anymore."

"We should do something," I mutter, but we're frozen.

Dollar Dan smiles at the spinning dog for another agonizing beat, and then drops him back on the ground. He says something, and the dog wags his tail, trembling.

The dog continues shaking while the snow beneath him turns bright yellow. After he's finished, Dan drags Stewart back up the driveway through the snow.

"Well, now I really don't want to go in," Libby says, handing me the binoculars and wriggling to create more space between our hips. "Did you see that? He just hanged his dog."

"We have to talk to him," I say, climbing back into the passenger seat. "Who knows, maybe he even has Ralph's Chewbacca head in there." I nod at the house. I explained the collectibles/auction thing to Libby on the way over.

"You're right." She reaches over me to check her reflection in the rearview mirror. "We've gotta get our heads on straight—we'll get him to show us around somehow and just . . . see what we see. Now remember." She fixes me with a look. "Change of plans this time. Dan's obsessed with you so I want you to play it dumb and pretty."

She pats my cheek. "The stupider they are, the stupider they want. Meanwhile I'll get the whole thing on tape." She flips through the apps on her phone until she finds a voice recorder.

"Dang," Dollar Dan says, sucking what looks like barbecue sauce off his chubby fingers. He's around five-ten, with a round face and small, dark eyes. I wouldn't call him ugly, per se. It's just that I haven't been so physically repulsed by a human body since our ninety-year-old neighbor Mr. Jenkins forgot to take his dementia medication and rang our doorbell in the nude. (He was a very nice man, but that doesn't change the fact that his balls sagged to his knees. RIP.) There's something about Dan that makes me want to run in the other direction.

Libby elbows me in the side.

Oh yeah. I'm supposed to flirt.

"Can we, like, come in, Dan?" I ask, batting my eyelashes. "It's sort of . . ." I glance down at my own chest. "Nipply out here." We rehearsed that line in the car. It sickens me.

"Oooh, a tit bit nipply?" He raises his eyebrows and

swings the door wide, leading us to a dimly lit room that smells like Buffalo wings and kitty litter. A TV is blaring in one corner—some kind of dirt bike contest. The trembling terrier is sprawled out on the dingy carpet, averting his eyes as the first bike crashes into sand.

"They hardly ever die," Dollar Dan says, staring at the TV. "Mostly they break their necks or their backs. It's lame."

Libby nods at me.

"Oh my Gah, yeahhhhhh," I say. "I wish it were cooler." I force myself to smile. "That would be so . . . *cool*."

He takes a step toward me, narrowing his eyes. I try to keep smiling, but it probably looks ridiculous. He smells like that sludge-green cologne that Davey used to wear in middle school, and my mouth is dry and acidic. I'm afraid I might barf.

He slaps me on the ass so hard I yelp.

"What're you doing here, Crazy Kippy?" he asks in a low voice that I'm sure he thinks is sexy.

I rub my stinging butt cheek and shoot Libby a look of betrayal. "Just, uh, wanted to see you," I manage to say.

"Dan," Libby says, like she's about to share the biggest secret. "The truth is that Kippy is dying to see your trophy collection."

"Right," I mutter. The burning in my ass has subsided. "I would very much like to see your sports awards."

Dollar Dan smiles goofily, staring straight at my boobs.

"Baby, Kippy, baby," he says, in this low gorilla voice, and so rapidly it's like he can't really control the words coming out. He may have had quite a few head injuries, come to think of it. "C'mere," he adds, reaching for my hand. "Trophy time."

I let him hold it. His fingers are sweaty and he smells like hot pennies. It reminds me of blood, and for a second I zone out a little.

"Kippy will be thrilled," I hear Libby say. "Look at how thrilled she is—well, that's just her face, but believe me, she's so excited."

Dan opens a door. Stairs leading to a dark basement.

"NO THANK YOU PLEASE," I yell, yanking my hand away. I blink at Dan and Libby, who are both staring at me, and shake my head. The dog barks sharply at the TV, and I think I smell blood again—grass stains, too. When Ralph was dragging me inside, there was so much blood. My blood. He stuffed grass in my mouth and pulled my broken body up his back steps—thump, thump, thump—and when he saw the bone had pierced my pants he knelt down to play with it. Davey came before he could drag me into the darkness of that cellar, but if he hadn't, I would have died underground, in the dank underbelly of Ralph's creepy house. I can still remember the pain of lying there, waiting for the basement to happen, for life to end. The pain was like lightning.

I wince, rubbing my thigh. "No basements."

"Come on," Libby hisses at me. "If you faint, I'll catch you."

"I'm not going to faint," I snap. "It's not, like, all I do."

"C'mere, baby," Dan says, pulling me forward. And for a second his grip is so strong yet gentle on my elbow that I forget why we came here and just follow him. It feels nice to be touched. If I shut my eyes I can pretend it's Davey's hand there, guiding me. I don't untangle myself from Dollar Dan until we reach the last step. I'm a terrible girlfriend, probably. I deserve whatever's waiting for me down here.

Downstairs, metal shelves run floor to ceiling, displaying Dollar Dan's various trophies and medals—except for one wall, which has been reserved for mounted animal heads. Reclining otters and electrocuted-looking squirrels are displayed alongside startled does and ten-point bucks. A pair of antlers hangs next to some medals. There's a whole basket of loose antlers on the ground.

"Whose necklaces are these?" Libby asks, running fingers along the gold trinkets strung around the neck of a mounted fox head. They all clink together like a grotesque wind chime.

"That's where I hang my chains," he says proudly. "My chains are for the ladies. But the ladies aren't here, in my house—" He looks at me and laughs. "Not usually. So when I'm at home I hang my chains on the animals." He thumps his chest. "I'm an animal, too, when it comes to the ladies."

"Ooh la la," I say. It comes out way too loud.

"Right," Libby says, crossing her arms. "So, Dollar Dan, where were you Friday?"

"How come you don't sound nice anymore?" he snaps.

She raises her eyebrows. "Excuse me?"

"You pushed me at school and now you're being a bitch. I don't know if I like you."

She rolls her eyes. "Dan, come on. Where were you on Friday?"

"Who cares?" he snaps, crossing the room to root around in the antler basket.

Libby glares at him, then leans in close to me and whispers in my hair, "I'm gonna go snoop for evidence. You said a Chewbacca head, right? Keep him talking."

Before I can choke out, "No, don't leave me," she's disappeared up the stairs.

I breathe in through my nose and out through my mouth, pretending to admire the trophies. What will I say when Dollar Dan returns from his weird bone basket? *Nice bones?* I just hope he doesn't try to kiss me. I have a history of not doing the right thing when people other than my boyfriend try to kiss me. (I mean, it only happened once, but still.) When Colt was in jail and I went to question him, he had some sort of feral-animal thing going on—he'd grown a beard and probably hadn't hooked up with anyone in weeks, which for him is like starvation. He yanked me against the cold bars, shoving his tongue in my mouth, and even though I felt nothing, I let it happen because part of me was like, *Huh. So this is what that's like.*

Something pokes me hard in the chest. I shake myself out of my memory-lane reverie and look down to see Dan stroking my left breast with an antler.

"Stop," I tell him.

"What? It doesn't count as my hand." He laughs. "Plus,

what do you care? You're just a dumb slut, right?" He pokes me so hard in the chest that it hurts. I take a few steps back, dumbfounded, frozen. "I know you want me," he says.

"Libby?" I call.

"Nuh-uh," he says, grabbing me by the front of my shirt. He yanks me in so close that his chin touches my forehead. He wraps one arm tight around my waist and I can feel the antler, still held in his other hand, digging into my spine. I slap at his chest, trying to remember that move Miss Rosa taught me—the one where you kill a man with a single blow—how did that go? Something about the nose bone . . . But I can't lean back far enough to slap his face. I feel the antler start to creep up between my legs.

"Dan," I stammer. "Don't."

I shove hard on his shoulder, but he shushes me.

I try to pinch my legs together but it hurts so I spread them apart again, and he shoves it up even harder.

"Does that feel good?" he asks, his voice low.

I shake my head, blinking away tears. I can't even talk. The swallowing feeling in my chest has teeth now. I'm starting to sink. I can hear a dog bark.

At Davey's house the dogs are barking, and I go in and I see him there above the counter and it's like—

"Fuck you, bitch," Dollar Dan says.

I am showing up at Mrs. Klich's house to talk to her about Ruth, and she is spinning dead above—

I am crouched in Ralph's closet listening to his footfalls on the stairs—

Dan is screaming. The antlers thud against the carpet.

"Fuck!" Dan shrieks, falling to his knees.

His hands are off me. I'm free. I kick away the antlers and scramble away from his writhing body. Why is he writhing?

"Are you okay?" someone asks.

I spin around to see Albus standing at the bottom of the stairs.

"No," I whisper, shutting my eyes.

When I open them, it's Libby.

"Are you okay?" she asks again. Her hands are shaking.

It takes me a second to connect Dollar Dan's pain with the sight of her. But then I see the knife sticking out of his butt. The one Miss Rosa gave her.

"I stabbed him," she confirms, nodding quickly. "I threw the knife at him and now it's in his butt so we should probably go."

"What the fuck, you cunt!" he yells. He is trying to reach behind himself for the knife but can't bring himself to touch it. I press my back against the wall, as far away from him as possible, and edge toward Libby. "Yeah, let's go," I say quietly.

But she pushes me away when I try to take her arm.

"That's my knife," she says, striding toward Dollar Dan and yanking the blade. He screams, and she screams. Blood spurts onto the carpet. The smell of it is everywhere. And then I'm screaming, too.

FRIENDLY BEASTS

"What the heck were you thinking, Libby?"
We're careening down Route 45—the only stretch of
road in Friendship where you can legally go over thirty-
five miles per hour. ("I need to drive fast," she kept saying as
we scrambled through Dollar Dan's snowy yard to her car.)

"That stuff's been going on since I was twelve," Libby
says. "Boys touching me like that's what I was born for."

"You mean like . . ." I trail off.

"No! Not like molestation. Not everything is an emergency. Jesus." She tosses her hair, glancing at the ceiling.
"Sorry, Gah."

"I don't get it," I stutter.

"Yes, you do, Kippy," she says. "You do. You were
standing there, and he was trying to tickle your hoo hah

with some old animal bone, and he thought it was sexy or funny, and how did you feel?"

"Scared."

"Exactly. I've been trying to look good ever since I first knew I looked good. I love makeup, and I love my body. Gah gave it to me. I gotta keep it hot. But you know what every single man who's ever met me since I was still a child thinks about it?"

I shake my head, glancing nervously at the speedometer.

"They think I do it for them," she says, one eye twitching slightly. "They think I wear a skirt because I wanna get hugged. Colt thinks I curl my hair so he can rake his fingers through it—do you know how long it takes to get a good curl? Teachers stare at me, my dad's friends have made jokes about me turning eighteen since I was thirteen, I've had a reputation for being a slut before a boy even tried to kiss me. Seeing Dollar Dan slap your butt in the hallways makes me remember every single time he's done that to me starting in middle school, when I first grew tits. And when I saw you crying just now while he tried to . . . Well, I'll be darned if I didn't know then how sick of it I was." She takes a deep breath. "I'm sorry I told you to flirt with him—not like that's what caused it. Gah, certain boys will come at you with antlers raised no matter what you do."

"Uh-huh." She's sort of rambling but I get the gist. Misogyny has ruled her life and Dollar Dan is certifiably nuts.

"Do you think it could have been Dollar Dan that night—going after Davey to get to me?"

"Maybe."

I root around in my backpack for the list.

1. Shadow man
2. Ralph voice mail
3. No blood alcohol
4. Bedroom display
5. Ralph is insane and capable of anything
6. Ralph is rich enough to pay an accomplice
7. Accomplice: needs to be either totally crazy or desperate enough for money to become crazy
8. Mildred's VHS tape: figures 1 AND 2

But who was the second figure? Who would be dumb enough to help an idiot like Dollar Dan? The speedometer climbs from fifty to fifty-five to sixty-five. I try to double-check the speed postings on Route 45. They're always changing based on the deer population—if there are too many deer, the speed limits drop to reduce human fatalities—but Libby's going even faster now and we're whizzing by the signs too fast for me to read them.

"Libby, slow down."

"Why? It's not like the police are ever—"

As if on cue, sirens scream behind us.

She groans. In the rearview mirror I can just make out the large yellow smiley face stamped on the hood of every Friendship squad car. It's got its lights on and it's headed right toward us.

"Uggggh," she says, pulling over onto the shoulder. "Well, that was fun while it lasted."

"Are you okay?" I ask, turning around in my seat, trying to see which cop it is. But it's getting dark outside, and the neon lights swirling atop the cop car are getting in my eyes. In the strobe-lit blackness, I think I make out a little girl.

Albus?

I swallow and turn back around. I'm seeing Albus more and more lately. The more stressed out I am, the more she's there, it seems like. "You were getting pretty worked up before, talking about boys—Libby, are you sure you're—"

"What?" She arches an eyebrow at me. "So you're the

only one allowed to have meltdowns now?"

"That's fair." I shrug. "I accept that."

I hear the police radio crackle through the window and put my head in my hands. "Ugh. Please don't let it be Staake," I mumble.

"Correction," Libby says, reaching into her purse. She seems surprisingly calm for someone who just stabbed a guy and is probably about to get a speeding ticket. "Let's pray it's Staake."

"God, Libby—"

"Gah," she warns, slathering her mouth in lipstick.

"What if Dan called the police?"

"Shh," she hisses, struggling out of her down coat. "Hold this." She chucks it at me. I hug it to my chest, watching her wrestle out of her heavy wool sweater. She chucks that at me, too, and starts rearranging her boobs under her camisole. Cleavage on the front lines.

Behind us, a car door slams.

"Whoever it is, he's wearing a balaclava," I whisper, twisting in my seat. "A camouflage one—Jesus, it's unsettling—I can't see his face." There's also a gigantic key hanging from his belt. It's Staake.

My stomach lurches and spots start swelling in front of my eyes. "It's happening," I hear myself whine. "We're going to jail. I can't do this again."

"I am *so* over your fainting," Libby says, still reaching into her camisole to hoist her boobs together. "I can't deal with you messing up my routine. Just pretend to be asleep or something."

Somehow closing my eyes and holding still makes me feel less dizzy. I'll have to remember this trick for next time.

Staake knocks on the glass, and icy air pours into the car as Libby cranks open the window.

"Well, hello, Libby Quinn," I hear Sheriff Staake say. "Aren't you a pretty peach this evening. Per usual."

I feel my face scrunch up. He never talks to me that way.

"Why if it isn't Mr. Sheriff Staake!" she exclaims.

"I'm gonna keep on my balaclava—that is, if you don't mind," he continues. "Blood vessels keep bursting all over my face from this dang cold."

"I sure hope you're having a blessed day, Sheriff Staake!" Libby chirps, sounding like a high society lady in one of those Southern films. "It was a pity we didn't get to talk more yesterday afternoon, when you swung by the Frieds'." Her voice is about ten octaves higher than her normal grumbly tenor.

"A real shame—say, is that Kippy Bushman over beside you?"

"Yessir. I took that poor thing for an afternoon drive and she fell straight asleep. You know"—she lowers her voice—"I think it might have something to do with all those pills her psychiatrist is giving her."

"Oh, it's mighty sad," he says.

"Mighty sad," she echoes.

"You two staying warm?"

"Yessir."

The truth is that it's freezing in here and I wish Libby would hurry up with whatever flirt maneuver she's doing because I'm having trouble holding still. My body wants to shiver. I can't even imagine how cold she is, sitting there in only a camisole.

"It's good that you're nice to her, Libby Quinn," he says. "Heck, I know it isn't easy for popular go-getters like you to be seen with the likes of that. I mean holy bajee-zus, would you look at her. Skinny like a dying deer. Hair unbrushed and crazy—like some kind of cotton-candy mayhem."

Libby does some verbal nodding.

"Skin like slush," he continues.

Okay, this is getting ridiculous.

"That girl needs a tan," he goes, grunting softly. "My Lisa takes a lot of care with her tans."

"You're right, Sheriff Staake," she says, "and you know

TanGlo over on Main Street is very good—I go there myself."

"As do I. Just because we're northerners doesn't mean we can't look healthy. It's not good to be, hmmph . . . Well, no offense, but your friend there . . ."

"I'll talk to her about TanGlo."

"You do that. Now listen." I hear the sound of paper rustling. He's probably bringing out his superofficial sheriff's notebook. "I noticed you were speeding—about twenty miles per hour over, Libby Quinn, and you know we're cracking down on speeding ever since that big collision yesterday."

"I'm sorry," she says, sounding about ten years old.

"Well, it's fine, I guess—but you know, I also got a call from Daniel Shully, over on Amity Street."

"You did?" Libby squeaks.

I keep my eyes squeezed shut. Now would be a bad time to get caught fake sleeping.

"I did. Now I'm sure there's been some kind of miscommunication, but do you wanna tell me your side?"

"Well, I showed up at his place unannounced—which was rude, I know that." She sighs. "But Kippy here has had such a big crush on Dollar Dan ever since he started playing football—you know how young girls are—"

"Oh, do I ever. I hear you girls call him Dollar Dan because of his nipples," Staake says, chuckling. "Looks like she didn't take long to get over Mr. Coma."

Libby laughs uncomfortably.

I grit my teeth.

"Well, anyway," she says. "We went over there and Dollar Dan was just going to show us his trophies, and what have you, which was real nice. But then we found out that his parents weren't home and . . . Well, I don't know about you, Sheriff Staake, but my father has a strict rule about parents always being there. Adult supervision is a must wherever I go."

"Oh, of course," Staake mumbles.

"So the minute we found out it was just Dollar Dan and us," Libby continues, "I told Dollar Dan we had to leave. I said we'd come by again when his parents were around, but I just couldn't stay without them there. My father would kill me. And then . . . well . . . Sheriff Staake . . . apparently Dollar Dan's had some kind of crush on me forever, and he thought that Kippy and me and him . . . Well, he thought . . ."

Staake grunts. "He thought it was going to be one of those threesome dealies, didn't he?"

"Yes," Libby blurts out, obviously relieved that he's telling the story for her. "That's exactly what he wanted.

I'd never even heard of them before. And when I said no, he had some sort of tantrum. He grabbed a hunting knife and threatened to stab himself if we wouldn't!"

"Oh my."

"I've never seen anything like it. It scared us so bad we ran away." She exhales. "Did he really do it? Stab himself, I mean?"

"What is going on with people around here?" Staake roars. "Everyone's heads are all mixed up. We used to be good Christian people."

"Tell me about it," Libby says. Her teeth are chattering from the window being open. "Honestly, sir, I just figured that what I learned tonight is Dollar Dan's own business. My parents always taught me that if someone isn't right in the head, it's not your beeswax, and I didn't want to go embarrassing anybody."

"Well, it sounds like you have the right idea—but next time someone tries to force one of those threesomes on you without your permission, you give me a call. Here's my card. A woman always has the right to say no, Libby, you remember that.

"Now my booty's freezing out here, and you look mighty, uh, chilly, too. So I think I'll let you ladies head out. I'll check in on Dollar Dan, and you keep an eye on Kippy Bushman. She means well." I listen as he walks away, and Libby quickly rolls up the window and turns the heat up higher.

"That's what a double D's worth of cleavage gets you," she hisses in my ear as Staake honks past us. I smile, reaching for my list.

"You're a real pro, Libby."

While she's focused on getting her coat back on I write:

9. Libby=official wingman

My phone buzzes in my pocket and I reach for it, hoping it's not another weird message from someone wanting to talk about suicide.

"Oh, Colt texted," I mutter, reading the alert. I programmed him into my phone so that I could have a backup number for my night with Davey.

"What'd he say?" Libby asks, sounding excited.

"Let's see," I mumble, opening the text. Probably some more fake sympathy about Davey. Colt never contacts me.

Text from Colt W. (mobile):
Yo McKetta, whatchu doin tonight? I wanna fuck.

"What is it?" Libby asks, pulling off the shoulder. "Read it to me."

"It was a mistake." I stuff the phone in my pocket. "It's nothing—"

"Kippy." She says it the same way she said *That's my knife* after stabbing Dollar Dan. "Is something going on with you and Colt?"

"No!"

"Then show me!" She jams her hand in my pocket, reaching for the phone, and nearly drives us into a ditch.

"Jesus," I snap, handing it to her. "Fine, take a look. It's the only text he's ever sent me, and it wasn't even intended for me."

She reads it over and over again. I grab the wheel a few times so we won't go off the road.

"Libby?" I ask finally. I expect her to hit the accelerator again—to drive us straight to McKetta's ranch house and run through the front door with Rosa's knife held aloft. Instead she looks crumpled in the front seat, weak and tired.

"It's kinda late," she says finally and firmly, taking the wheel. "Can I . . . can I sleep over?"

I tell her yeah. It's the least I can do.

I'm psyched, to tell the truth.

Dear Lampy,

I'm writing you because it means I'll have something to give you when you wake up, which means that you'll wake up. (Magical thinking.)

Also I want to say something to you: SURVIVE! For me, it's the exact same thing as saying something else that rhymes with "By Dove Boo"—which I would never say to you right now because I don't want to jinx anything, because I feel like as soon as the universe knows how I feel about you, that's when it will take you away. (More magical thinking.)

I mean, what do you even say in these situations when you're trying to not be too mushy or melodramatic? Get well soon?

Anyway I better go. Libby invited herself to sleep over. She says it's because we have more work to do, but honestly I think Dollar Dan scared the shit out of her. Not to mention she's gloomy about Colt, who cheated on her—though she says it doesn't count as cheating because they were never "official."

Personally I don't care what the label is, because if you like someone you're going to be possessive of them no matter what.

And yes: I am bringing this up as a way of saying that A.) I am possessive of you. B.) I have not hooked up with anybody else since you went to intensive care, which was admittedly only the day before yesterday. Also C.) I am secretly worried that you will wake up when I'm not there and forget who/where you are and wander into the hospital room of some pretty girl and accidentally cheat on me. ☹

I mean, let's face it: anyone would hook up with you, Davey—especially a gorgeous girl with terminal cancer who might never see a hot man again unless she believes in heaven/angels/sex things in the afterlife.

My paranoid fantasies tend to be really epic lately.

I'M GOING TO FIND OUT WHO DID THIS TO YOU. (Revenge fantasies.)

Love,
Kippy

HARK!

"Enjoy those cookies," Dom says, all breathless, winking at us as he shuts my bedroom door. He started baking stuff as soon as I walked in and asked permission for a sleepover. I guess he's relieved that I'm back to normal kid things like slumber parties with non-male characters.

I roll my eyes at Libby. "He's usually meaner than this," I insist, tossing her a pair of onesie pajamas that I'm pretty sure will fit her in the boobs. "Especially lately. That was basically the first time he's spoken to me in twenty-four hours." Recaps of parental bloopers feel exaggerated when there isn't proof. "He interrupted my therapy session and got stuck in all of my trip wires. I think it changed him."

Libby rolls her eyes. "I don't know what that means,

but one time my dad walked in on Colt and me dry humping and next thing I knew Pastor Bill was at the house like I needed an exorcism or something."

My jaw drops. "Did they actually do an exorcism?"

"No, Lutherans don't do exorcisms. Pastor Bill just stood there feeling awkward while my dad turned red. I kept trying to explain that we weren't even doing anything—at least not what my dad thought we were doing. But it's sort of hard to make a case for yourself when they've already made up their minds."

I choke on a piece of burnt cookie. Dom tries very hard and wears very frilly aprons, but unfortunately he's not very good with recipes, so every single cookie is burnt and hard enough to crack a tooth on.

"Right?" Libby starts changing into the pajamas I gave her. She buttons the shirt to her neck and expertly removes her bra through one of the sleeves. "Seriously though, Kippy, we need to talk about these." She nods at the tray of homemade sweets. "They look like coals for a fire—not even my dog could digest them and she eats her own poop."

"Maybe try sucking on them? That's what I usually do. It softens the charred layers enough to eat. We can flush the rest down the toilet." Downstairs the Christmas music starts blasting.

I put one of the rock-hard cookies between my lips like a lollipop. The ashy taste brings to mind carcinogens, and memories. "So, Libby," I say, smacking my lips. I haven't had a sleepover since before Ruth died, and I'm not really sure what you do at them. I think Ruth and I spent a lot of time laughing? "How are you this evening?"

"Um, fine, I guess," she says, staring at me sullenly. "My boyfriend's cheating on me but other than that I'm okay.

"I know what you're thinking," she says. "He wasn't my boyfriend."

"Not at all." I toss the cookie back on the blackened pile, trying to think of something slumber partyish to distract her. "I could braid your hair?"

"Okay."

"I don't actually know how."

"Then why—"

"Sorry."

She sighs. "Let's talk about me. I just . . . I know this is pathetic, but I'm, like, wondering what I'll do now. Because I obviously . . . I don't want to get back together with him. Or whatever . . . I mean, how did I actually think Colt would be a good boyfriend when the whole reason we got together in the first place was him cheating on his girlfriend? Duh, Libby." She wrinkles her nose and takes the cookie out of her mouth. "These are really bad."

"Yeah, they're gross."

"But all my friends are his friends. I mean, they're not even my friends, they're just girls I drink with or cheer with. They all love him, I think, secretly." She plays with the carpet. "Where am I going to sit at lunch now that I'm never talking to him again?"

"With me," I say.

She smiles a little.

"I was worried about the same thing after Ruth died, if it makes you feel any better. I thought my first reactions would be . . . I don't know. Bigger, but they weren't. Sometimes I even forgot to be sad. Sometimes I *hated* her." I rake my name into the carpet. "It made me feel like a sociopath, but I was, like, who am I going to stand with in the hallway now?"

She glances up at me, nodding a little.

I shrug. "I'll stand with you."

She beams. "I have an idea." She reaches into her humongous purse and pulls out the bottle of vodka she snagged yesterday from Davey's.

I get up and lock the door. "What are you, Mary Poppins?"

"Who?"

"It's open, for Pete's sake—if Sheriff Staake had searched your purse you would have gotten a huge ticket."

"Oh please," she says, twisting off the cap. "Sheriff Staake's too obsessed with my boobs to even remember what a ticket is." She thrusts out her chest. "Everyone's distracted by these guys—my own dad hasn't been able to make eye contact with me for seven years. Now let's get drunk and tell each other secrets. Here"—she holds out the bottle and nods—"tell me something that nobody else knows."

I cradle the bottle with both hands. "Like what?"

"Something really crazy."

"Okay." I glance at the list peeking out of my backpack. Davey's attacker is still out there, but we can figure out the next step tomorrow. Even professionals have to take breaks.

I take a sip and force myself to swallow. Fire fills my stomach. I've never done this before. "Low-judgment zone?"

"Low-judgment zone," she agrees.

"The night they arrested Ralph, before the cops showed up, and it was still just me and him, I peed my pants," I say, wiping a noodle of drool from my chin.

Libby ogles me. "Like full-on?"

I nod, bracing myself to faint, but the admission feels

more like a script than a memory. I should probably go easy on the vodka—I mean, I guess this is why Davey used to drink. It lets you remember without thinking you'll die.

"So what?" she snaps, suddenly enlivened. "You had an accident. Don't beat yourself up about it. You thought that dickwad was going to kill you and drink your blood. Every time I've gone hunting the animal has messed itself before it stops bleeding." She flaps her hand at me like it's all so casual.

This is what it feels like to hang out with girls, I remember—there's this very specific, very intoxicating kind of female support that I've learned to forget. Now that it's back, I realize how much I missed it.

"Hey, look at me." She pokes my knee and I do. "Animal fear is part of animal instinct—at least that's what my mom says when we're hunting, to remind me to respect the prey." She shrugs. "Pissing yourself is a part of the same science that lets you survive."

I roll my eyes, mostly to keep the tears in. "You make it sound like I'm brave."

"Oh, shut up," she snaps. "You so are." She wiggles her fingers for the bottle. "My turn."

I hand it to her and she takes a long glug, then slams down the bottle and exhales.

"So here it is," she says finally. "I've heard that if you give more than twenty blow jobs you don't get into heaven." She takes a deep breath. "And I've given twenty-three."

I hold my face very still, trying to be respectful.

"Where did you hear that?" I ask.

"I Googled it."

"You Googled how much oral sex you can—"

"Yes, and there were a lot of different numbers, so I averaged them. And then I rounded down, because I figured rounding down would be the most conservative thing, mathematically. Colt wanted to push it to twenty-four, and I just—I couldn't. I kept imagining the . . . you know"—she flutters a hand at the ceiling—"the flames."

"Hellfire?"

"Yeah. And it's probably why he started cheating on me today with Sarah McKetta."

Tears fill her eyes. Now would probably be a good opportunity to tell her that the McKetta thing has, according to rumors, been going on for a while—probably long before the blow-job decision—but I don't want to upset her.

Oh, let's be serious. Despite everything I promised myself, Libby and I are sort of becoming friends, and I don't want her to know I kept it from her.

She scoffs. "In case you're wondering, it's time for you to reassure me."

"Colt's a jerk," I snap, feeling genuinely angry on her behalf.

"Thank you!"

"And honestly, Libby," I add, gaining steam. "I mean, I don't know if this makes you feel any better, but I completely understand your need for rules. I had all these rules laid out for my first time with Davey. I had flash cards and schedules mapped out. I had outfits picked. I wanted to wait until I got my cast off, because I thought it would look better—even though, you know, deep down I didn't *really* want to wait. Like, in my gut I'd been raring to go for a while.

"Honestly? Not to diss your religion or anything, but I think the rules we make for ourselves are more about fearing rejection than fearing mistakes. Colt totally fucked up, but if you and him make up, or whatever—or if you meet someone new, and you really want to give him a blow job, or, I don't know, *get* a blow job—then maybe you should just go for it. And if you don't want to because of some rule you've come up with by averaging a bunch of random numbers and combining them with Bible stuff, maybe it's because you don't particularly trust that person, and maybe you should listen to that."

"I guess part of it *was* knowing he'd tell everyone," she says gruffly.

"Whoever you're with should feel lucky, not entitled. Right now Colt might be the only person in this town who's up to your physical standards—"

"He is," she says, sighing. "Compared to him, the men in this town look like garbage animals." She glances at me guiltily. "No offense to Davey."

"None taken because he's objectively the hottest person I've ever seen, no offense to Colt."

She smiles.

"Anyway, just think how many other people there are in this state, or even in the country, or even in the world," I continue. "What if you, like, studied abroad one year? You could go anywhere and find anyone. Colt isn't your only option."

"Guys in Brazil are really hot, I've heard."

"Fine."

She makes a face. "But I've also heard they wear thongs."

"Kippy!" Dom yells from downstairs. "Food's ready!"

"One sec," I tell Libby, climbing to my feet.

It takes Dom and I awhile to arrange the utensils, napkins, glasses of milk, and bowls of macaroni on the breakfast-in-bed tray. "Can we have some orange juice, too?" I ask, thinking of the vodka.

"That tray's gonna be too heavy for you to carry," he says.

"I got it, I promise."

"I was thinking of going to Rosa's tonight, then swinging back in the morning so we can all go to the Frostbite Challenge. Can I trust you two ladies to—"

"Dom, come on," I say, cutting him off. He's giving me the weirdest look and for a second I'm worried he's going to say something about Libby and me having sex. (I'm sick of fighting with him about sex I'm not having.)

"No séances," he says instead.

"What the eff?"

"Don't sass me, Miss Pickle," he says, crossing his arms. "I know what today's youth gets up to, with your bonfires and witchy-craft and eyeliner and things." He looks so old and out of it in his pink frilly apron that I almost start to cry. "Don't fool around with the devil, is what I'm saying."

Up until right now I had no idea that Dom even believed in the devil. "Okay," I tell him, nodding hard. He looks so concerned about the occult that I can't even tease him.

I turn and trudge up the stairs.

"Sorry that took so long," I shout, huffing up the last few

steps. Months in a cast will make you super out of shape. "Apparently my dad believes in magic." I turn the corner to my bedroom and set down the tray on the carpet.

"What's going on?" I ask stupidly. Libby's gotten dressed. Her purse is packed and the vodka is gone.

She holds up my most recent letter to Ralph and slings her purse over her shoulder.

I shut the door behind me. "You went through my backpack?"

"'She's busy singing along to Beyoncé, which is kind of ironic when you consider the fact that the lyrics are mostly about self-empowerment and Libby's stuck cater- ing to Colt's every whim,'" she reads aloud. "'I mean, we're not really *friends* or anything—she's sort of just my driver—but if we were, I'd definitely tell her about the rumors that Colt's hooking up with Sarah McKetta.'"

I open my mouth a couple of times but can't think of how to explain.

"'Libby's a pretty good wingman,'" she continues reading, "'but—well, you've met her. Her boobs are big- ger than her brain and she's so used to getting what she wants, she thinks the answers are gonna fall straight from heaven.'" Libby stares at me, furious. "What exactly does it take, Kippy Bushman? Do I have to be ambidextrous or say *thrilling* or *brilliant* instead of *cool* for you to think I'm not retarded? Do we all have to be atheists and skip grades and go around acting awkward and, like, soooooo over it to be smart like you?"

"I do think you're smart," I say quietly.

"Thanks." Her eyes narrow like this is the worst possible thing I could have said. "You're the most selfish person I've ever met," she says. "I used to make all these excuses for you in my head—I used to think you were autistic or something, I felt bad for you, but now I just think you're a dickhead."

"I was going to tell you about McKetta, really, but—"

"But what? But you decided it was easier to not mess up your ride situation?"

"I didn't even know we were friends! You kept saying that you were only hanging out with me because of . . . Gah and—"

"Have you ever hooked up with Colt?" she asks. I can hear the garage door opening. Dom's leaving for the night.

"What?" My heart pounds

"Have. You. Kissed. Colt." She crosses her arms. "Be honest because I'll probably find out anyway."

I should have told her sooner. During one of the many times that she apologized for her behavior after Ruth died, I should have said, "Listen, we all make mistakes—this one time when I went to see Colt in jail . . ." I should have mentioned how repulsive I found it so she would know I wasn't trying to date him, or something.

"It was nothing, and it was forever ago," I plead now. "Well, it was, like, two months ago. But you and I weren't even nominally friends yet, and he and I were both crazy. Ruth had just died." Tears prick my eyes and I swipe at them, hating all this. "I'm not—look, just because you find him hot doesn't mean everybody does. Personally I find him repulsive." It doesn't come out the way I wanted it to.

"I wasn't even going to send that letter to Ralph—I just wrote it so that I could go on thinking of you as a tool. You know so I wouldn't . . . get attached." Nothing comes out like I want it to.

"Nice." Her lip curls. "You're such a flipping hypocrite. All your ladies-liberation bullcrap. You go around saying I should be empowered, and then you talk behind my back, calling me a bimbo, talking about my tits—even I talk less shit than that. Maybe I'm more of a feminist than you. You think you're so much better than everyone, and that you're in this great relationship. But how great can it really be if Davey tried to kill himself?"

I want to sit down. I want to go back in time to before Dom called me downstairs, back when I was still giving

Libby advice, and she was listening, and we were both in my pajamas.

"I made up the blood-alcohol thing," she says. Her voice is flat, dead, but her mouth is still smiling. "I played along because I knew you were weird about investigations. You're always talking about how you solved Ruth's murder—"

"I did—"

"And I felt obligated to take care of you," she continues, raising her voice, "to make things right with her, so I made up the blood-alcohol thing, and I shoved some vanilla candles and some of my mom's roses in my purse thinking I could stage some kind of romantic scene at his house and when you and I went there I stuck them in his room."

"Why?"

"Because I didn't want you to think he'd killed himself to get out of having sex with you!" She hoists her bag up higher on her shoulder. "Everyone knows he's only your boyfriend because he feels sorry for you. Why else would somebody date Crazy Kippy?"

"You write letters to serial killers," she says, shoving past me. She gives me a quick look like *those are the facts* before storming down the hallway toward the stairs.

Big stupid tears are rolling into my mouth.

"Libby, come back—"

"You spy on innocent strangers," she shouts from the stairwell, stomping down the steps. "You hook up with your dead friend's boyfriend, and then when that doesn't work out, you go after her brother, and *then* when *that* doesn't work, you let some big-nippled freak fuck you with an antler."

"Go to hell," I yell, but she's already slamming the front door.

I wait for Dom to shout out, "Is everything okeydo-key?" so that I can wail, "No!" and have somebody comfort me. But then I remember he's left already.

"Fine," I scream to no one, slamming my own door so hard that I hope Libby can hear it from the driveway. Then I sit down on the carpet and cry until I think my body will break in half. Everything bad has happened, everyone good has gone, but so far nothing has hurt worse than the realization that I am irreparably and irrefutably insane.

1. Shadow man ??
2. Ralph voice mail
3. ~~No blood alcohol~~
4. ~~Bedroom display~~

5. Ralph is insane and capable of anything
6. Ralph is rich enough to pay an accomplice
7. Accomplice: needs to be either totally crazy or desperate enough for money to become crazy
8. Mildred's VHS tape: figures 1 AND 2
9. ~~Libby=official wingman~~

I'm crazy

I'm crazy

I'm crazy

I'm crazy

GO TELL IT ON THE MOUNTAIN

Ralph and Albus and I *are sitting on a tiny twin bed at Cloudy Meadows, laughing about something. We're wearing those pajamas—the ones without any drawstrings so that we can't hang ourselves. Albus tells Ralph that her real name is Adele Botkins, but that he should call her Sir Albus. They get on the floor and use crayons to draw a map of the basement so that I can escape.*

"You go ahead," Ralph says. He's making cocoa now. "We'll stay here."

Before I leave I tell Albus I'm afraid he might hurt her. She puts her little hands on my face and says, "You're going to be great and I know it."

"How?"

"Because I'm not crazy, Corporal, and neither are you."

I can see the door leading out of Cloudy Meadows and know

I'll be safe if I can just get through it—but then I see Davey in our living room. "They made it look like a home," I say, running toward him. "You've got to come with me. We need to warn people."

Albus is screaming, being murdered. I know I have to make a choice and I choose Davey.

He grabs me and kisses me. Christmas carols are playing on Dom's stereo.

"Did you know this is my favorite song?" Davey whispers in my ear. "The lyrics are like Ativan."

I forget what I was rushing for. "You like the part where they sing, 'Fall on your knees, O hear the angel voices,'" I say. "You told me before, when you were alive—"

I hug him because I'm sorry.

We laugh. He's still alive.

"'O hear the angel voices'—but are they angels or devils?" he says. "Who are you falling on your knees for? Who are you vulnerable to?"

"Now there's a question for English class." I want to change the subject. "I'm vulnerable to you," I say.

He hoists me up around his hips so that I'm hugging him like a koala bear. "The song means you have to listen to the crazy stuff inside your head, Kippy." He squeezes me too tight. "Crazy Kippy."

What crazy stuff? I want to ask him.

What voices in your head? I want to say.

But he's squeezing me too tight.

I can't breathe.

I jolt awake, my head wedged between two couch cush-
ions, and check my phone. It's only ten p.m. The pills
must have made me doze off.

I didn't try to kill myself or anything. (I guess that's one
way to figure out you're not suicidal: You find pills, you
take the doctor-prescribed amount, and you don't want any
more.) It's just that after hating on myself for however long
following Libby's weird departure, I felt like I was having
a heart attack/falling into a volcano, and also like maybe I
was going to do something I'd never done before, something weird and "counterproductive" (to put it lightly), like
dig my nails into my own arm or break my hand punching
the wall a million times. So I tore through the medicine
cabinet and found an old prescription bottle of Ativan from
Dr. Ferguson, from when I first got out of the hospital. I
popped a double dose (*Take 1–2 per day for panic attacks*, the
bottle read) and sat on the couch in front of the TV, nodding
at the evangelical channel before eventually falling asleep.

I feel great, actually. Or at least I don't feel like the
world is ending. The thing about Ativan, I guess, is that it
makes you look at yourself and say, *I* understand *that you
might* feel *like you're covered in magma, but it's not real magma,*

the magma is in your mind, and it's going to pass.

Also: *You made a mistake and you need to apologize to Libby. But crossing a few things off your evidence list doesn't mean the whole investigation is kaput.* The Ativan said that, too.

I smile. *Thanks, Ativan.*

Then I pick up my cell and dial Jim Steele's home number.

"Hullo."

"Hi, Jim?"

"Kippy?"

"Were you asleep?"

"No," he says groggily. "Just a little drunk and watching the evangelical channel."

"Me too—well, minus the drunk part." I decide not to tell him about the Ativan. "Weird."

"Yes, that is why I like the evangelical channel," he says. "Because it's weird."

"Any news on the Chewbacca head?"

"Oh, that." I can imagine him rubbing his own head. "Yes. I'm meeting the guy tomorrow. He wouldn't give me his name but I plan to throw a lot of legal mumbo jumbo at him and get the head." He yawns. "I'll, uh, tell you if I recognize him or anything."

"Yeah, and any distinguishing features—even if they're personality based." I pull out my list and ignore the cross-outs. Libby might have been right about me being a bad friend, but that doesn't mean she's right about everything—or that she was even telling the truth necessarily about half the stuff she said.

In a business like mine, you can't trust anyone.

1. Shadow man ??
2. Ralph voice mail
3. ~~No blood alcohol~~
4. ~~Bedroom display~~
5. Ralph is insane and capable of anything
6. Ralph is rich enough to pay an accomplice
7. Accomplice: needs to be either totally crazy or desperate enough for money <u>to become crazy</u>
8. <u>Mildred's VHS tape: figures 1 AND 2</u>
9. ~~Libby=official wingman~~
~~I'm crazy~~
~~I'm crazy~~
~~I'm crazy~~
~~I'm crazy~~
10. Accomplice: good with computers/ sneaky

I don't know if Dollar Dan would necessarily be smart enough to *not* give his name to an interested buyer online. But does that rule him out as a suspect?

"Kippy?" Jim says.

"Yeah, sorry, did you say something?"

"I said, 'Are you going to the Frostbite Challenge tomorrow?'"

I swallow. Libby and I had talked about going together and I feel a hot rush of self-loathing come over me.

But then it passes.

Thanks, Ativan.

"Yeah, I think I'll go," I say.

"I'll be there for when they announce the winners. We can discuss the whole Chewbacca-head thing then."

"Cool."

"Cool," he says, imitating me.

"Whatever."

"Whatever."

"You're drunk."

He sighs. "I am. Good night, Kippy Bushman."

"Night."

I put down the phone and snatch the remote to switch off the TV. I can only take so much evangelical channel before it stops feeling like an anthropological study and starts sounding like church, which I couldn't deal with after Mom died. I think back to what Dom said about the devil. Has he always been so weird, or is he just starting to seem weirder because I know what a weirdo *I* am?

I flip through my phone to check my email. I've got one new message.

From: Nita_Fried@memail.com
To: Kippyyyyyyyyyyyyyyy@memail.com

Hey sweetie,
Surprised we haven't heard from you yet—though of course that's on us, too. We've been in such a tizzy about Davey, as I'm sure you can imagine. You probably already know about the visitor's list. We wanted to put you on it but the ICU has a policy about family. Obviously we'll keep you posted, and honey, do feel free to call.
Xo,
Nita

"Huh?" I mumble. What does Mrs. Fried mean she hasn't heard from me? I wrote back to her first note right away. I search for her name in my email and two separate addresses pop up. There's the one she just wrote me from (which is the one she usually writes me from) and NitaFried3000@hotwahoo.com.

> We've been dealing with Davey's mental health
> issues as a family for a while now, and we find
> a certain comfort in doing so privately. Please
> understand. Davey had been deteriorating mentally
> for months prior to this most recent cry for help.

Mrs. Fried has the tendency to be a little cold, but that email was so unlike her.

Who was emailing me from the hotwahoo address? Who even uses hotwahoo anymore?

Probably whatever creep went after Davey. And potentially whatever guy Jim Steele is going to meet tomorrow.

There's only one way to find out.

I punch the fake hotwahoo address into a new email.

From: Kippyyyyyyyyyyyyyy@memail.com
To: NitaFried3000@hotwahoo.com

Dear Mrs. Fried,
I think I know who hurt Davey. Meet me at the
Frostbite Challenge tomorrow and I'll give you

the name . . . maybe the police will listen to you
instead of me.

KB

The whole town will be there. That's almost seven
hundred people. Hopefully I'll be safer in a crowd.

A new message comes through almost immediately.

From: NitaFried3000@hotwahoo.com
To: Kippyyyyyyyyyyyyyyy@memail.com

4 o'clock?

I take a screenshot and text it to Mrs. Fried. I cut out
the part about whoever hurt Davey because I don't want
to frighten her. She'd probably call Staake.

Text from Kippy (mobile):
Mrs. Fried, thanks for your email earlier! I'll call soon.
PS: Is this from you?

I zone out to TV for a while—some *Twilight Zone* epi-
sode about a guy making a pact with a demon for more and
more money, but his life just keeps getting worse and worse.

My phone buzzes.

Text from Nita Fried (mobile):
NO, NOT ME! DOES THIS MEAN I'M BEING
CATFISHED?!?!

Text from Kippy (mobile):
Probably just spam! Thank you for your email. . . .

Text from Nita Fried (mobile):
XO SEE YOU SOON, DAVID MISSES U

She attaches a picture of Davey, completely unconscious in the hospital bed with tubes coming out of him.

I cringe. *Parents.* Then I take a deep breath and write
back to the mystery emailer: Sounds good.

I know that Ralph doesn't have access to email in
prison, but I just know in my gut that he's behind this.
Whoever's helping him on the outside—whoever's
responsible for Davey's current state—could have created
this fake address to throw me off the scent.

I take another look at my list.

1. Shadow man ??
2. Ralph voice mail
3. ~~No blood alcohol~~
4. ~~Bedroom display~~

5. Ralph is insane and capable of anything
6. Ralph is rich enough to pay an accomplice
7. Accomplice: needs to be either totally crazy or desperate enough for money to become crazy
8. Mildred's VHS tape: figures 1 AND 2
9. ~~Libby=official wingman~~

~~I'm crazy~~

~~I'm crazy~~

~~I'm crazy~~

~~I'm crazy~~

10. Accomplice: good with computers/ sneaky
11. Fake emails: first one arrives after visiting Davey in hospital/seeing Sheriff Staake at the Frieds' house (why did he forget his gun??). Second one arrives night before FB Challenge, confirming meet-up. Conclusion: whoever is behind the emails will be at Frostbite.

I tap my pen against the crinkly sheet of paper. If I'm right, and the fake emailer is the same person meeting up with Jim Steele tomorrow, then I've got to warn him. He's pretty street smart, but who knows who we're up against?

I redial him on my phone, but it goes straight to voice mail. He must have passed out.

"Um, hello, Jim?" I say as soon as it beeps. "I'm not very good at messages. Just uh, be careful tomorrow, okay? I know you think I'm crazy about this, but . . . I don't know, maybe you shouldn't go at all. I mean, maybe you don't need to. I think the same guy is coming to meet me, so . . . call me in the morning or something."

I hang up and put the phone in my lap. Dom disabled all my booby traps after Dr. Ferguson came, and I'd probably be feeling really shitty about that right now except the Ativan has taken all my bad feelings away. I watch *The Twilight Zone*, idly thinking about devils and friendship and whether Davey's tubes hurt until my phone buzzes in my lap and I snatch it up. The automated recording for the Green Bay Correctional Facility blares in my ear.

"Ralph," I say once I can hear him breathing. Not even drugs can slow my heart rate.

"Kippy," he says, drawing out the word for so long that I think *he* must be on drugs or something. "I thought I'd call because a friend of mine just relayed a message. Apparently you received a special email. Congratulations,

Kippy. I'm so happy this is going the way I'd planned."

"Ralph, who is it?"

"Who's who?"

"Cut the crap. Your guy on the outside. The one who's selling the Chewbacca head. The one who hurt Davey. Is it Daniel Shully? Dollar Dan? Was it your idea for him to try to, like, rape me with those antlers?"

"What did this person do, exactly?" Ralph's voice is dark, empty.

If his guy on the outside is *not* Dollar Dan, I can imagine that Ralph might encourage whoever is helping him to *kill* Dollar Dan.

"It's nothing. It was just a misunderstanding with antlers," I mumble.

"How do you know it's a guy, Kippy?" He draws out my name even longer this time. "As far as I know, Davey hurt himself."

"Please," I whisper. I remind myself that Dom always locks the doors when he leaves. We have kitchen knives and blunt objects, and hypothetically speaking, I know how to kill a man with one swift upward movement to the nose. But even with the Ativan, my heart is racing. "You can tell me. I won't get you in trouble." I rack my brain. What does one say to woo a narcissist? "You've already won, Ralph. Telling me doesn't undo that. Think of Davey, think of Ruth." I feel sick. "Think of all you've accomplished—"

"Shhhhh," he says, and it's silent for two whole commercials while I wait for him to finish.

"This isn't happening, Crazy Kippy," he whispers finally. "None of it is real except for in your mind."

It's quiet again, but this time he doesn't come back, and when I look at the phone there's no active call, just the screenshot of Davey that I keep as my background photo and the little swipe thing that says *Unlock Phone*. I have to check my incoming calls to remind myself that this one really happened.

Blocked Call at the very top.

I call Jim Steele's voice mail again and remind him to be careful.

SEE, AMID THE WINTER'S SNOW

Dragons, pirates, angels, elves, a cow that looks like Satan, a cow that looks like a llama, a ten-foot-tall replica of Sheriff Staake's face. There's even a gigantic smiling mouth full of perfect teeth, carved by the local Friendship dental hygienists.

"Good turnout," Dom says, surveying the Frost-bite Challenge fairgrounds with approval. "I'll go get us drinks."

I nod, busy rereading the texts on my phone.

Text from Jim Steele (mobile):
Got ur messages. I am fine, thank u. Will cu at FBC. $$$
☺ $$$

I already texted him saying, "Cool," or whatever. But I decide to text him again. It might be annoying, but I'm starting to get worried.

Text from Kippy (mobile):
Hey, what's ur ETA?

Then I decide to text Libby. I drafted and deleted a million messages to her last night, but she's probably here somewhere, and I'm going to run into her, so I should at least acknowledge I was wrong before that happens.

Text from Kippy (mobile):
I should have told you about Colt. I should have told you what people were saying about McKetta. I should have thanked you better for the rides, and for protecting me from Dollar Dan. I should not have said those things about you to Ralph. I am sorry. I wish I could take it back but I can only learn from it. You are kind and smart and loyal and you inspire me to be a better person. Please be my friend!

It's very corny but it's all true. I write and delete the line "Please be my friend" approximately a zillion times before finally going "Agh!" and pressing Send.

"Pickle!" Dom shouts. He waves at me from the drink tent. "You want cocoa?"

I shake my head and shuffle past the giant ice sculpture of a Green Bay Packer's helmet to roam around until I find Libby's piece in all its glory: Jesus on the cross, every thorn on his crown perfectly defined. Her dad is perched on a stepstool, still chipping away at the gash in Jesus's side. Technically every participant is allowed to continue working until the bell sounds tonight at six, at which point all the judges come out and everyone gets drunk.

"Where's Libby?" I ask her dad.

"Oh, she'll be here," he says, like he doesn't know who I am. Or maybe he's just focused on the spear wound. Or maybe he *does* know who I am and is playing it cold because he thinks I'm a real jerk.

I reach up to scratch my face through the balaclava. I'm wearing it for warmth, per usual, but also to disguise myself so that whoever's coming to meet me will have to look around a little, giving me time to ID them. "Merry Christmas Eve," I tell Mr. Quinn. He nods, his attention still on Jesus.

"Hey, Pickle," Dom says, coming up behind me with hot chocolates.

"Thanks," I say, taking the cocoa. "How did you recognize me with my balaclava on?"

"Um. Because I came with you and you're my daughter?"

"Right."

"So you're meeting up with some friends?" He scratches his head, looking around like he's bored. "Because I was thinking of taking Rosa—"

"Go." Usually I'd be annoyed by how much he prioritizes their time together. But I can't exactly stealthily stake out the fairgrounds with my loud, talkative father yapping about his feelings, and how cold it is, and what sorts of ice sculptures folks made "way back when." (*Some of these very same folks, don'tcha know! Ed there used to be a princess guy. Now he builds turtles. Who'd a thunk.*)

"Rosa and I will meet you at the picnic tables for the judging, okay? Someone built a maze out of ice and we wanna go smooch in it."

"Cool, thanks for letting me know."

He pulls me in for a hug and kisses my face through the balaclava. "I'm sorry for everything, Pickle," he says before taking off without specifying which of the many things there is to feel sorry for. The thing that sucks about family is you're stuck with them no matter how good they are at saying sorry, so you just have to accept their apologies in whatever shape or form they come in. It makes me wish that Libby were my sister or my cousin or something. At least then I wouldn't be sweating into my snowsuit about whether she's going to return my text. If we were related, we could fight all the time, and I could be like, *Oh, she's mad at me now*, and I could accept that while knowing that it would pass—that it would have to, because we'd be at the same barbecues for the rest of our lives or whatever.

Ugh, I wish I had taken Ativan this morning. Unfortunately I tossed it down the toilet because I didn't want to become a drug addict; part of me was like, *You know what's better than a heart-racing life? An Ativan life.* And then I started to understand why Davey likes drinking and the whole thing got really scary.

I roll my eyes at myself and walk off to blend in, thinking about the heart that Davey was planning on carving. There are hundreds of sculptures out here, and lots of them are hearts, but none of them are anatomical like the one he wanted to make.

I pass a family with three kids chipping away at a family of crudely made ice mermaids. To my right there's a gigantic duck sculpture, and next to it, the icy personage of a man posing with a gun (it might be a cowboy, or it might be Sheriff Staake). While onlookers edge by me, weaving between sculptures, chomping on their brats and slurping cocoa, the ice sculptures themselves reflect the flashing red lights of the ambulance, parked in reserve near the exit, just in case someone gets too drunk.

Something slaps me on the butt and I jump.

"Hey, hottie," I hear Colt say.

I spin around and twist his finger until he screams. "You!" I snap. "You are the reason that Libby and I could not pass the Bechdel test and once again ended up enemies." Okay, so mostly it's my fault that we had a falling-out. But I still want to *scream* at him.

"What??" he yelps. "It was a compliment!"

"So, now that I'm off crutches you think it's time to initiate me into ass grabbings?"

"Kippy? I didn't know it was you—you have a fucking balaclava on." He wrenches his hand away. "I thought you were Libby—you were just talking to her dad, for fuck's sake. What do you want from me?"

"Why would Libby want you touching her ass, either?" I snap. "You accidentally sent that text to me yesterday, you know. She knows about McKetta."

"Um. Okay." He laughs, casually flicking his fingers like I barely hurt him. "You're acting like me and her are together or something—"

"You ruined my night last night, did you know that? You ruined what could have been a beautiful sleepover-y end to a difficult day."

"What are you, a lesbian?" he whispers. "Maybe mind your own business and stop being such a bitch."

"You're the bitch." I jab a finger at his chest. "You're the weak and dumb and mean and slutty one. You think you're so powerful because you're surrounded by all these pretty girls—and you want them so you think it's reciprocal. Did it ever occur to you that you're projecting? We're not responsible for how you feel about us. We're not witches!"

"Shit, quit being so full of yourself, Kippy. I never said you were pretty."

"Oh my God. That's seriously what you just took away from the most articulate monologue of my life? Listen, Colt, if you don't want a piece of this"—I gesture at my snowsuit—"then why did you just touch my ass five seconds ago? You can't confuse me."

Colt looks confused. "I'm gonna tell Libby you're crazy and she shouldn't hang out with you," he says, backing away.

"Too late," I shout. I cackle maniacally to myself before slinking back into stealth mode. They've plowed the excess snow to the corners of the grounds, creating giant mounds. I climb one to watch from, pulling out Mildred's binoculars and checking my watch: ten to four. Ten minutes until I'm supposed to meet whoever was posing as Davey's mom. If Dr. Ferguson could see me now he'd say

I was being paranoid. But I know the truth. I'm the only one who knows the truth.

I train my binoculars on the crowd of people moving through the fairgrounds, trying to pick out familiar faces. There's Libby, joining her dad by their Jesus. Sheriff Staake. Pastor Bill.

Then I see Dollar Dan wearing a long black coat and combat boots, dragging poor Stewart by the leash. He's glancing up and down the fairgrounds like he's looking for someone.

I adjust the magnification so I can see him better.

He's looking right at me, smiling.

I thought that meeting up in a highly populated spot would be safer. But now I feel like surrounding myself with hundreds of potential murderers might not have been the smartest move.

"Yo, Kippy," someone calls.

Everyone's pointing and shouting about something. I swing my binoculars.

"Kippy!"

I jump. It's Mildred, barreling toward me. "I was looking for you."

I try to hike farther up the snowbank but slip and slide down, ending up right at her feet. "How did you recognize me with my balaclava on?"

"Because your hair sticks out the bottom and you dress funny in a way I remember. Hey." She flashes me a weird look. "We need to talk."

My heart feels like a brick in my chest. Could Mildred be the fake emailer? I look around to see if anyone's watching us. Ralph did say that it wasn't a man. At the time I thought he was just messing with my head again, but—

"Like now," she says. "We need to talk right now." She grabs my arm. She's just gone through a breakup, and she's a little unstable, and she's definitely obsessed with Davey—but is she weak enough to be Ralph's email puppet? There's a psychopath on the loose and now this woman is yanking on me, trying to get me to follow her to her car.

"No," I yell. Crowds of anxious families pour around us. A megaphone whines in the distance. "Everyone remain calm," a robotic voice instructs.

"What's going on?" I ask, tugging my arm away.

Something flashes in my peripheral vision and I glance over my shoulder, thinking I see Albus again on her bike.

I shake my head, willing my brain to cooperate, but the ice sculptures are beginning to loom larger than life around me, smiling at me just like Dollar Dan.

I finally wriggle from Mildred's grip, slipping into the

crowd to escape. "Kippy!" she shouts. There's a ring of police officers huddled near an ice sculpture of a mermaid. They're all standing stock-still—fixated on who knows what. I don't have to tell them everything, but maybe one of them could just give me a ride home so Dollar Dan doesn't smile at me again and Mildred doesn't kidnap me.

"Dammit, Bushman," Staake's voice booms overhead. "You stop right where you are—"

As he scrambles down the metal bleachers, his feet slip out from under him and he lands with a thunk on his butt, dropping the megaphone.

I shuffle closer. "Excuse me?" One of the cops turns to see me and blinks. Behind him, the ice is drenched in blood.

I push my way into the circle.

There in the snow, buried up to his neck at the base of the mermaid's tail, is Jim Steele.

"Jim?" I say, looking around at the cops. "Well—don't just stand there—somebody wake him—he'll get hypothermia." My words sound sped up. The mermaid sculpture glints in a way that makes my eyes hurt.

I fall on my knees, digging at the snow with my mittens. One of the cops grabs me by the elbow and pulls me to my feet. The snow I raked has streaks of red in it. Jim's face is a bluish color and a deer antler is protruding from his neck. Brownish gunk is stuck in his beard.

"But I just talked to him," I say dumbly. "He sent a text."

His chin tilts slightly—and at first I think he's waking up—but then his cheek hits the snow.

It's just his head.

WHILE BY MY SHEEP
I WATCHED AT NIGHT

A few hours later, Dom, Miss Rosa, Dr. Ferguson, and I are all sitting around Dr. Ferguson's dining room table, drinking wine, zoned out to the max. The three of us kind of invited ourselves over because he lives really close to the Frostbite Challenge fairgrounds, and Dom was freaking out and projecting all over Rosa and me and thought it'd be good to be around "a mental health professional who is also our dear friend, don'tcha know." Everybody's too in shock to say anything about the fact that I've poured myself a glass and won't stop talking about antlers.

"Did you know that the skin on a deer's antlers is called velvet?" I ask. "It sounds very pretty but it's actually full of veins, and when it sheds there's blood everywhere."

Rosa smiles sadly at me. "Shut up more."

"Fine." I take out my list, hoping that reviewing the facts will temporarily quell the swirling in my chest.

1. Shadow man ??
2. Ralph voice mail
3. ~~No blood alcohol~~
4. ~~Bedroom display~~
5. Ralph is insane and capable of anything
6. Ralph is rich enough to pay an accomplice
7. Accomplice: needs to be either totally crazy or desperate enough for money to become crazy
8. Mildred's VHS tape: figures 1 AND 2
9. ~~Libby=official wingman~~
~~I'm crazy~~
~~I'm crazy~~
~~I'm crazy~~
~~I'm crazy~~
10. Accomplice: good with computers/ sneaky
11. Fake emails: first one arrives after visiting Davey in hospital/seeing Sheriff Staake at the Frieds' house (why did

he forget his gun??). Second one arrives
night before FB Challenge, confirming
meet-up. Conclusion: whoever is behind
the emails will be at Frostbite.
12. Antlers
13. Dollar Dan had antlers. Lots of them.

I look up. "I have to go check on something. Can I
borrow someone's car?"

"No," Dom says, sounding very much himself even
though his face is sagging and he looks a zillion years
old.

"Okay," I mutter. Maybe I can just call Dollar Dan and
figure out whether he's guilty that way. Or maybe I should
call the police. Then again, maybe the truly right thing to
do in this moment is just chill out a little bit. It only seems
right to think about Jim. If I got beheaded, I'd want someone to sit there and think about me, and let themselves
feel it a little.

But then I do let myself feel it, and it's awful—like a
stabbing, breath-stealing sensation in my lungs.

I close a door in my head and reach for the bottle.

Dom wordlessly slides it away from me and downs my
glass of wine in one gulp.

"No," he says again.

"I just can't believe it," Dr. Ferguson says.

"Dr. Ferguson, would you mind if I locked all your doors and laid a simple trip wire in the front hallway?" I ask. "I would also like to use your phone." I could always call Green Bay Correctional to check on Ralph. If they have caller ID they would see the call was coming from Dr. Ferguson and they must let inmates speak to their doctors, right? And if he gets on the phone, I might be able to get something out of him about Jim's murder. Hearing his voice is always the creepiest thing ever, but he does like to admit things.

"Kippy," Dom says, his teeth purple from wine, "enough with the traps."

"You can lock the doors if you want," Dr. Ferguson says. "And feel free to use the phone—there's one in the guest bedroom, if you need privacy."

"Thanks." I push back from the table and go to lock the front door before sort of losing track of where the other doors are (am I drunk?) and making my way down the hallway, past the guest bedroom, to Dr. Ferguson's office. I like it in there. I'm used to it. The chairs are those big leather ones with the tufted arms. It looks a lot like his office did at Cloudy Meadows, actually.

There's a stack of receipts on the desk and I idly pull a few toward me. One is handwritten, from a place called

Scheidegg's Storage. I lift the receiver but stop with it halfway to my ear as I read the receipt. The dial tone hums. Pain yawns in my chest.

Scheidegg's Storage
3818 Route 135

Receipt No. 149-214
Storage Unit 189 [Ralph Johnston]
New owner: William Ferguson
Transfer of ownership fee: $12.99
First month's deposit: $60
Total: $72.99
Transfer Status: Confirmed

"Can I help you with anything?" a voice asks.

I turn around to see Dr. Ferguson blocking the door.

I hang up the phone. "No, I was just going to call my friend and say Merry Christmas Eve," I say weakly. "But I don't need to anymore."

His eyes shift to the receipt. I edge past him and dig in my pocket for my phone, trying to think if there's anyone out there I can still trust. Mildred was acting weird at Frostbite—almost like she was trying to abduct me—and Libby's mad at me, but maybe—

Text from Kippy (mobile):
Libby SOS—come get me 12 Mirabelle Road HURRY
BRING KNIVES & GUNS & WHATEVER I'M SO SORRY 4
BEFORE HELP ME

Text from Libby (mobile):
OMGah kippy ur still doing this???

Text from Kippy (mobile):
will u come

Text from Libby (mobile):
DUH

I careen into the dining room feeling feverish. Dom is sitting on Miss Rosa's lap sobbing again about Jim Steele. I can hear Dr. Ferguson's footsteps behind me.

"Guys, we gotta go."

Dom struggles off Miss Rosa, looking shocked. The blood is draining from his cheeks.

A hand clamps down on my shoulder.

"Everybody stay calm," Dr. Ferguson says, pulling me toward him. Something cold and metallic presses into my temple.

"What are you doing?" Dom asks, slurring his words.

"Put that down, Will, that's my baby. . . ." His lips are trembling.

I look away. If Dom cries then I'm really going to lose it.

"Phones on the table," Dr. Ferguson says.

I watch their phones clatter on their plates.

"Yours, too." The gun presses harder into my skull. I toss my phone on the floor.

"He's working for Ralph," I blurt out. "I mean, if we're all about to die, you should know the truth—" I scream as my elbow is grabbed and twisted. Pain radiates down my shoulder.

Dom's face is pure terror. Tears stream down Miss Rosa's cheeks. Dr. Ferguson cranks my elbow harder. The ache swells and ricochets through my clavicle, about to explode.

Rosa pleads with Dr. Ferguson in Polish. My shoulder pops and I wail louder.

Dom grabs a knife from the table and runs toward us.

My eardrums explode, everything rings, Dom is on the floor. I fall on my knees. My nose twitches from the blood. I know I should crawl toward him, but I don't want to see. My father is dead, I think.

But then he gasps, his breath sucking in all panicked, and he lets out the biggest scream I've ever heard. I've heard deer cry out like humans after getting hit by cars, and it was nothing like this.

Blood everywhere.

"We're going to the basement," Dr. Ferguson says.

Ferguson reaches for my sleeve and I recoil from him, wincing as I try to move my shoulder. My heart shrivels into a raisin. "No," I plead.

I scramble for my backpack and manage to loop it onto my good arm.

"*Ojcze nasz ktorys jest w niebie, swiec sie imie Twoje.*" Miss Rosa's eyes are closed in prayer. "*Przyjdz krolestwo Twoje, badz wola Twoja—*"

"Rosa," I yell, wanting to shake her.

Ferguson grabs me by the collar.

"We need to stop the bleeding," I mumble, letting Dr. Ferguson pull me backward through the kitchen to the basement door. His gun touches the side of my face as we walk.

I don't want to look at the staircase. I can smell the dankness, but I don't want to see the darkness. "Hello?" somebody says. It's a tiny voice, faraway.

I slide one foot and then the other onto the top step. The door slams behind me, hitting my shoulder, and I grip the banister. I will wait right here to die if I have to, but I will not walk all the way down. I might have braved Dollar Dan's basement, but that was for investigative purposes.

And at this point the investigation is over. At this point it's about where I want to die. "I am not getting killed in a cellar," I say quietly. I will die on the stairs.

"Why?" the tiny voice says.

"I don't know why!" I shout.

I will die talking to myself.

The door opens behind me and I turn to see Dom leaning on tiny Rosa, his arm wrapped tight around her shoulder, dragging his hemorrhaging leg as she struggles to support his weight. His pants are soaked through. The blood is purple-black.

I squeeze against the wall to let them pass, putting a hand gingerly on Dom's shoulder.

"No idling on the stairs," Dr. Ferguson growls, and kicks Rosa in the back, sending us flying.

The door slams above us as we land in a pile on the concrete. Dom is screaming again. Rosa is struggling to catch her breath. She got the wind knocked out of her. I cradle my forearm to my chest. My collarbone has already started to swell. I'm covered in Dom's blood.

"Are you okay?" I ask, not sure which of us I'm talking to, exactly.

"Is my back," she says, standing up and wrenching her torso left and right, cracking her whole spine. "There." She sighs and wriggles out of her sweater and turtleneck, fashioning a kind of tourniquet on Dom's leg.

"You okay, Pebble?" she asks me, tightening the shirt around Dom's thigh. He hisses through his teeth.

"My shoulder's dislocated," I say, sweat pouring down my face.

I reach for Dom's hand. "I'm so glad you got shot in the leg," I blurt out, squeezing his fingers. "I know that's weird to say, but I thought it was your intestines, and that you were about to turn inside out in front of me, and on the bright side you probably won't bleed to death now, or at least not as fast."

"Kippy," he whispers. His face is gray and his eyes are closed.

As Rosa fiddles with his bandages, I lean in close. "Yes, Dommy?"

"Silence."

Upstairs, Dr. Ferguson is rummaging through the cupboards, probably trying to brainstorm ways to get rid of our bodies. Apparently I'm the kind of person who sociopaths get obsessed with, which makes this all my fault.

"I guess you were right about the devil," I mumble.

"Kippy," someone whines. It's the same high-pitched voice as before.

I shake my head hard. I'd like to enjoy these last few

moments with Dom and Rosa without voices in my head getting in the way.

"What's that?" Dom says groggily, struggling to sit up.

I blink. "You heard it?"

Rosa wraps her arms around him. "Shhh, Kitten." She looks up at me. "Help me. We move. Hide in dark from gun man."

I don't want to move any farther into the basement, but I nod, linking my good arm under Dom's armpit to help drag him across the concrete floor. The only light down here comes from a tiny dormer window that looks out onto the ground outside. It's half-covered by snow. My eyes adjust slowly, and through the darkness I can just make out a lump in the far corner that looks like a pile of rags. Shelves line the wall, piled with stuff. There's a huge freezer under the staircase that reminds me of the kind Jim Steele used for his taxidermy.

Used. Past tense.

"It's me," the rags say. "Albus."

I shut my eyes and open them again, but she doesn't disappear. Rosa is looking back and forth between Albus and me, flashing funny looks.

"I've been looking for you everywhere," Albus says, sounding exasperated.

"Is that a chain around your ankle?" I ask.

She nods grimly. "Affirmative."

I shuffle toward her, digging in my backpack past the crumpled sheets of paper until I find the knife Miss Rosa gave me. I try to cut through the iron cuff on Albus's ankle, but I barely make a scratch.

"Stop," Rosa says. "You make it not so pointy." She sighs. "Even now I pray we stab the doctor monster."

Miss Rosa drags Dom over and we all sit around Albus. I explain to Dom and Rosa who Albus is, and then I tell Albus to start from the beginning. "I think I see you everywhere," I say.

Rosa and Dom search my face, looking worried. Albus grins. "I dream about you all the time."

"This is so weird."

Dom still doesn't get it—he's blinking like a confused kid. "What the—"

"Shh," Miss Rosa says again, stroking his face. "Stay awake, but quiet. You will need your muscles."

"Dr. Ferguson let me out before they fired him," Albus explains, still beaming at me. "It was the only nice thing he ever did." She wrinkles her nose. "Even though I'm pretty sure he discharged me because he hoped that I would kill you. I talked about you all the time, and how I wanted to be family with you, and how in a perfect world it would be nice if we had the same blood—and I think he thought that meant I wanted to see your blood, or something." She shakes her head. "He really doesn't like you. He kept saying that the only way to get better was for me to find you and finally do whatever it was I desired to do. He called it exposure therapy. Little did he know I just want to have a slumber party. And now here you are!"

"Wait, what?" I ask, deciding to ignore the blood thing. "Dr. Ferguson retired. They didn't fire him." I reconsider everything that's happened. "Oh. Of course they did." I shake my head. "He hated me this whole time. He wanted me dead."

"Why would anybody want to kill you?" Dom asks shrilly.

Miss Rosa grunts. "Everyone is wanting to kill Kippy. This is her destiny."

"Some lawyer got in touch about a lawsuit they were building, and apparently the big bosses at Cloudy Meadows freaked out," Albus says. "I heard the nurses talking about it. You were going to be a big problem for everyone, and they blamed him for you, and they thought it would look better once the suit went public if they could say they'd fired him—that's what the nurses were saying, anyway." Albus frowns. "Then they sent me home. I didn't want to go home. I told them, but they wouldn't listen because I was a minor. And Dr. Ferguson had changed all the paperwork to make it look like I was wrongfully incarcerated, too."

"I don't get it," I tell Albus. "You ran away and came here? I thought your family moved to England."

"To England? Nah, they live a few towns over. I already told you, I dream about you. I've been looking for you everywhere. As soon as I could, I ran away from home to find you. I couldn't remember your last name, but I knew about your friend, the one who died, so I found her name in the papers and looked up her family in the yellow pages. I thought they could tell me where you lived. I went home, got my bike, and I rode it thirty miles."

I think of the little girl's bike on its side in Davey's yard. "Jesus."

"Yeah," Albus says. "Anyway, I was about to ring the doorbell at the Frieds' house when Dr. Ferguson came around the corner taking off his hat. I recognized him and was like, 'Hey, Captain Ferg! What a coincidence!' but instead of answering he scooped me up and threw me in his trunk. Weird, huh? I was so pooped that I decided to take a nap in there and when I woke up I was chained to this pole."

"You've . . . changed," I say slowly. When she was my roommate, Albus was childlike—generally more imaginative than insane. I guess riding your little girl's bike thirty miles through snow and getting hypothermia and then being chained to a pole can probably alter a person's personality.

"You too!" she says. "You're even prettier."

"Who's changed?" Dom asks, completely out of it.

"Is he okay?" I ask Rosa.

"No," she says, like this is the stupidest question in the world.

"You need to buck up, soldier," Albus is saying. "This is probably bringing back a lot of your trauma from the last time. Ralph and all that. How he tried to drag you into his basement. You probably hate it down here, don'tcha, Corporal?"

I glance at her. How does she know? Was that part in the papers? Dom wouldn't let me read most of the news.

"But the fact is: you're our most able-bodied person," she continues. "We need you to be brave."

"But I don't even know what's going on yet," I say feebly.

"Then figure it out," she says. "It isn't that hard."

"Just tell me."

"Think."

I retrieve the torn list from my backpack.

1. Shadow man ??
2. Ralph voice mail
3. ~~No blood alcohol~~

4. ~~Bedroom display~~
5. Ralph is insane and capable of anything
6. Ralph is rich enough to pay an <u>accomplice</u>
7. Accomplice: needs to be either totally crazy or desperate enough for money <u>to become crazy</u>
8. <u>Mildred's VHS tape: figures 1 AND 2</u>
9. ~~Libby=official wingman~~

~~I'm crazy~~

~~I'm crazy~~

~~I'm crazy~~

~~I'm crazy~~

10. Accomplice: good with computers/sneaky
11. Fake emails: first one arrives after visiting Davey in hospital/seeing Sheriff Staake at the Frieds' house (why did he forget his gun??). Second one arrives night before FB Challenge, confirming meet-up. Conclusion: whoever is behind the emails will be at Frostbite.
12. Antlers
13. Dollar Dan had antlers. Lots of them.

"Ralph knew about what Dollar Dan did with the antlers, and he could have told Dr. Ferguson . . . and Dr. Ferguson would have known exactly what to say to get to me, because I went to him with all my fears. He knew I was worried Davey would start drinking again. He knew to pose as Davey's mom in those emails because I've always thought she was weird for leaving so much after Ruth died—he knew I was biased against her." I look up at Albus. "And you were the second person Mildred saw on her video. . . ."

"Like I said, Private, he carried me off to his car."

"Does he hurt you?" I ask suddenly, thinking of Libby's freak-out and the way men are.

"What?" She shakes her head at me. "No, that's gross. He's been really nice to me. It's actually been great. I've slept a lot and he made me lasagna yesterday. He gave me all these old blankets. It's way better than at Cloudy Meadows, to be honest. I've even got my own room." She gestures expansively at the dank basement. "I think he's planning to kill me at some point but keeps putting it off."

She glances at Dom's blood-soaked pants. "But I guess he's gone sort of insane now, huh? Tonight might be the night." She smiles at me. "I'm glad I got to see you before we die, Kippy."

I start screaming. Rosa and Dom stop hugging for a minute to join in, yelling for help.

Albus shushes me.

"Don't bother," she says, repositioning her rag blankets. "I've tried a million times. I think it's soundproof."

She reaches into her sweater, pulls out a red whistle, and blows into it so hard that my eardrums hurt. "See?" Dom and Rosa keep on screaming.

"How much has he told you?" I ask Albus, straining to be heard over the yelling.

"I dunno," Albus says. "He seemed pretty happy about this hairy head that he brought down today."

The Chewbacca head.

"He also brought down the entire lower half of a dead man," she continues, smiling, "no head, just the lower parts. At first I thought it was a werewolf he killed, because of the furry head, but then I remembered those are fake."

Dom quiets down and Rosa murmurs something to him. He stutters, pale from blood loss.

I put a hand on his shoulder.

Jim's body is down here somewhere. Probably in one of those freezers.

"There also might be something in those letters." Albus nods at a box under the stairs. "He brought some down today, and when I asked him what they were he wouldn't answer me—just gave me more lasagna and sauntered off. I tried to look at them already but my chain isn't long enough. Oh well."

I'm not exactly inclined to open up the creepy freezer, but I do drag out the box Albus indicated. As soon as I take off the lid I recognize the letterhead. "They're from Ralph."

"Dr. Ferguson talks about Ralph constantly," Albus says. "He tells me Ralph is his ticket to everything. He talks about you guys, too. Like, I really can't believe you're here because he genuinely hates you. He rants about it. He says you got him fired, made him broke. He's, like, bankrupt or something. He's planning to ruin you." She rubs her ankle, still smiling at me. "I told you he hated us."

"We gotta get out of here," I mutter. I glance at the dormer window but it doesn't look like it opens, and it's pretty small. I scoot under it to read the letter in the moonlight.

This letter was mailed from the
GREEN BAY CORRECTIONAL FACILITY.
Please report any misconduct to this facility.

Doctor,
As you know I'm writing this during our session
because they record our sessions SO NOSY
and this way I can tell you what you need to

know without them DRIPPING BOOGERS ALL OVER US. (Get it? NOSY?)

I'm VERY GLAD you've made the right decision. After selling my <u>PRICELESS COLLECTIBLES</u> your money woes should be gone, gone, gone!!!!

TAKE ALL OF MY THINGS!!!!

All I ask is that you help me tie up a few loose ends.

DAVEY FRIED emasculated me in front of Kippy, and ruined what could have been a very artistic ending to my friendship with her. It won't be hard. He has a weak spot for beer. I'm sure you have access to medicine. <u>NOW READ BETWEEN THE LINES.</u>

<u>YOU MUST AGREE</u> UP FRONT to deal with any hubbub that arises. <u>I DO NOT DABBLE IN BUSINESS WITH WEAKLINGS, YOU SEE—SO SORRY. This means that if anyone gets nosy, you take care of it.</u>

<u>KIPPY, oh sweet Kippy. I know you have your own vendetta against her, but keep her safe for now and at my say-so. I want her to FEEL, do you understand. SHE'S SO BEAUTIFUL WHEN SHE DOUBTS HERSELF,</u>

DO YOU NOT AGREE? Bring her to the brink of crazy, and leave her there.

Just those THREE THINGS, Doctor, and you won't have to worry about your lost income anymore. I have enough money to set you up for life.

YOU'LL SEE WHAT I MEAN!

Ralph

"Ralph paid him to hurt Davey," I mutter, passing the letter to Dom, who's using Rosa as a backrest. They look like a bobsled team. "He must have been pissed that I was happy. But then who did I see at Davey's?" No one, I guess. My heart pounds.

"Kippy," Dom says, his fingers shaking as he reads the letter. The skin on his hand is rough with dried blood.

Rosa reads the letter, too, and growls.

"Jim told me he was going to look into who was auctioning off Ralph's stuff," I mutter. "He was going to bully them into handing over the cash. He didn't know it was Dr. Ferguson." The words feel heavy. I should never have baited him to go.

"Collateral damage," Dom whispers.

"Hey, Private," Albus says, nodding at the window. "You've got a visitor."

A shadow passes on the other side of the glass.

I would recognize those snow boots anywhere.

"Libby," I shout, climbing onto a folding chair to bang on the glass with my good arm. She ducks down, gawking at me.

"Oh my Gah," she mouths.

Just then the ceiling starts to vibrate.

"What is that?" I yell, straining to be heard over the noise. I recognize the whirring sound from the Frostbite Challenge.

"Chainsaw," Albus shouts. "You better hurry up and save us, Corporal."

Rosa's glasses slide down her nose from sweat. "Is time for traps." She scrambles to her feet, reaches behind her, and pulls her bra through one of her sleeves. "Straps!" she says, wiggling her fingers at me.

I step on the folding chair and turn around, gingerly holding my bad arm so she can unhook my bra. She ties mine together with hers and grabs some of Albus's blankets. "I build snare," she grumbles, barreling up the stairs.

Libby is banging at the glass with the butt of a rifle. Glass fractures overhead, crunches, and breaks.

I open up my eyes to see her clearing away the shards with a sweatshirt.

Upstairs, the chainsaw has stopped and the doorknob is rattling.

"I tie shut door, Doctor," Rosa yells. "Is because I hate you!"

"Hi," Libby says, beaming at me. "I got your text and I accept your apology. I Googled how to forgive someone without letting them, like, fully off the hook, and there was an eHow saying that 'I accept your apology' is better than 'It's okay'—"

"Libby—" I jump up and toss my knife through the window. Libby leaps to avoid being sliced by it. "That's great, thank you so much, it's just I don't really have time to explain so can you just pull me—"

"Wow, you're, like, really dirty," she says, grabbing one of my hands.

"Can you call Sherriff Staake?"

"My phone's dead. I can't call anyone!" She tugs on my good arm and I feel my feet leave the ground. "But I *did* call the Teen Tip Line before it died and left a message." She sounds proud of herself. "So we'll be okay."

"They probably check that, like, once a week!"

"I'm glad we're friends again. Also, Davey *just* woke up. Another thing I sort of lied to you about was that I gave a bunch of doctors my number when we were at the hospital—what?" She grunts, trying to pull me the rest of the way through. "Don't look at me like that—they were cute. One of them called before and told me about Davey opening his eyes, but now my phone's dead—whoa, good thing you're skinny cuz this window's teensy."

"Davey's awake?!"

I turn sideways, wriggling like a fish even though I can feel glass cutting into my flesh, and then the cold air hits my face like a million long-awaited pinpricks.

"Davey's awake." A smile cracks my chapped lips. Libby hands me the knife I tossed through. I squeeze it in my hand, nibbling my lower lip. "He's alive." Blood trickles down my skin.

"Gah, you look awful," she says, flinging snow off her fingers. "What's even happening? Why did you tell me to bring this?" She picks a rifle out of the snow and holds it up like, *Hello?*

I shake my head hard. I have to focus. "Dr. Ferguson shot my dad and threw us in the basement."

"Ew."

"Also my shoulder's out of joint," I say, shivering. "He did that, too."

"I'll fix it—one sec," she says, sticking her head back in the window. "Come on," she shouts into the basement.

She groans and pulls, leaning back on her heels.

Miss Rosa's head pops through the hole, but the rest of her is wedged tight.

"I too fat," she says, blinking blindly at the night sky. "Leave me."

Before I can stop her, Libby lowers Rosa back down.

"No," I yell, pulling on Libby's coat. "He'll kill them."

"Kippy," Albus calls. "Your dad's asleep. You better hurry."

"There's no time," Libby says, handing the rifle down to Rosa.

"I help!" Rosa calls out from down below. "I shooting his butts off!"

Libby grabs my elbow and shoves my arm upright in the socket.

I scream, thinking she's broken it. But then it doesn't hurt anymore.

"There," she says. "I do it for all the girls on the team."

"Thanks." I pull a shard gingerly from the soft part of my stomach. "Do you have any more weapons?"

"I've got the knife Rosa gave me."

"Good. Okay, come on."

I lead her around to the back porch, watching from the shadows as Dr. Ferguson tries the basement door a couple more times, then gives up and starts splitting the wood with his chainsaw. "You're better at throwing than me," I tell Libby. "So I'll distract him and you go around to the other side and disable him."

She nods. "Just like with hunting deer. We'll corner him." Before I can nod back, Libby pulls me in for a bear hug.

"I'm sorry," she says into my hair. "I should have believed you." She squeezes me so hard I choke. "You're crazy but not, like, chainsaw crazy, and you were right."

"I accept your apology," I croak, gazing over her shoulder. Inside, splintered wood hangs off the basement door like scabs. The chainsaw sputters to a stop as Dr. Ferguson takes a moment to yank the fractured pieces from the frame. "We gotta stop hugging now though."

"So we're okay?"

"We're great," I say, pulling back from her. "I'll be the decoy." My teeth are chattering and it isn't from the cold. "Don't be scared," I say, totally projecting.

She scoffs. "Oh please." But you can tell she's nervous, too, by the way her knees knock together as she runs off.

I wait to bang on the sliding door until I see her silhouette in the kitchen. Then I thump hard until Dr. Ferguson puts down the chainsaw and looks over his shoulder.

I step back into the shadows. His eyes are right on me, but he's so backlit that he can't see a thing. Libby's got to throw the knife while he's distracted—before he sees her. She's got a perfect shot.

He grabs his gun off the counter.

"Shit—come on, Libby," I whisper. "Come on."

She's just standing there in the doorway, her knife clutched at her side.

"Don't freeze," I plead, trying to will her to go through with it.

I watch her bite the tip of her tongue in concentration, aiming, the knife gripped in her fingertips.

"Go," I hiss, trying to will her to hurry. "Throw it."

She takes a step forward, bracing herself—and she must make the floorboards creak or something, because he turns around and sees her.

I see the gunfire before I hear it.

Then Libby's on her knees, clutching her stomach.

I crank open the door and he whirls back around to face me. I throw Rosa's knife as hard as I can, aiming for his skull.

It lands with a squelch, buried to the hilt in his right thigh, and he hits the ground with both knees. Before he can reach for the gun I do a roundhouse kick to his face, then swipe the gun across the hardwood floor with my foot, picking it up in one hand. I train it on his head, stomping toward him.

"Don't," he says, as I kneel down beside him. "Please."

I press the barrel against his nose and press my foot against the knife's handle until he's sobbing. "Give me your keys," I growl. "And your phone."

He wrestles them out of his pocket. I yank out the knife, grab the keys, and scramble to Libby, colliding with Rosa.

"What took you so long?" I ask.

"Holes in door are small and I must wiggle." She's gripping Libby's rifle with both hands. I offer her Ferguson's gun, handle first, afraid I might kill him with it. She takes it from me and aims both weapons at the doctor.

I fall on my knees next to Libby. "Look at me," I plead, fumbling with the zipper on her down coat. A slowly expanding circle of blood is seeping into her sweater.

"Hey," she gulps. Her teeth are covered in blood. "Am I—"

"You're great," I assure her in a panicky voice, struggling with the numbers on Dr. Ferguson's cell. The buttons are swimming before my eyes. My fingers are slippery with blood.

"I am wanting for to kill you, Mister Doctor," Miss Rosa is saying to Dr. Ferguson, wagging the gun at him while he cries. "I am wanting to explode your brains like melon on floor. You are devil."

"Nine-one-one operator, what is your emergency?"

a merry voice inquires.

"I'm at Twelve Mirabelle Road. We're shot and beaten. How long will it take you to—"

"Now hold on, miss, slow down—"

"We're dying!" I shout, watching the color drain from Libby's face.

"Okay, now just keep talking to me, don'tcha know, we'll get EMTs on their way. Things are going a bit slow tonight, what with the Frostbite Challenge and that whole decapitation thing, but we're up and running, you betcha."

I shake my head, unable to speak. This isn't like last time. They can't just walk me through CPR like when I found Davey. By the time they get here it will be too late.

I hand the phone to Rosa. "Here, talk to them," I beg. I wedge the phone between her bloody cheek and shoulder.

"Hello? Is Rosa," she says into the phone. "Soup is on."

I race to the door of the basement and barrel down the stairs, leaping over the body of my father, who's still groaning, thank God.

I kneel down to unlock Albus, flipping through Ferguson's keys until I find the right one. "You gotta help me," I tell her. "It's bad and I can't carry Libby or my dad by myself. We gotta get them into the car."

"You can do it," she says. "You can do it yourself, General."

"No," I snap, dragging her with me. "I'll come back for you, Dommy," I yell as we rush past, even though he's out cold. Upstairs Rosa is still training both guns on Dr. Ferguson, who's clutching his leg and glaring at us. "Can I shoot him head?" I hear Miss Rosa asking the dispatcher. "No? Okay, is fine."

I kneel beside Libby, trying to wriggle my arms under her body without hurting her. Her face is chalk white. "The keys to your truck are in your coat, right?" I ask her.

"They're in the ignition," she whispers. The veins in her neck are black and pumping visibly. Her eyes flutter closed and panic hits me like lightning.

"Albus, help me!" I beg, straining to lift Libby's dead weight. I look up to see Albus smiling at me from the kitchen.

She shakes her head. "Sorry, Lieutenant, but I gotta run or they'll return me to my parents. Being stuck in Dr. Ferguson's basement was a dream come true compared to home."

"Albus, that's—"

"Crazy?" She grabs a handful of meatloaf from a pan on the counter and shoves it in her mouth. "I love you, Kippy." She gestures with her red whistle. "If I need you, I'll toot."

She disappears out the back door.

"Albus!" I scream.

"Who are you talking to?" Rosa demands, covering the phone.

I keep yelling her name until Libby raises a sticky hand to my face.

"Kippy," she says, swallowing. "Pray."

"I don't know how."

"EMTs say half hour!" Rosa yells. The whole room is fading. "I am powerful," I say softly. "I am beautiful." I unlock the front door and race back to Libby, repositioning my arms underneath her. In my mind, my feet are tree trunks growing into the floor. I have the arms of a bear and the heart of a lion. I am a dinosaur. I am Kippy Fucking Bushman.

I plant my legs and lift. My heart is pounding so fast that I can hardly feel the pain shooting through my legs and arms. Rosa is shouting something but I cannot hear her. My mind is fast and Libby is light.

"Survive," I command Libby, who's gone now, fast asleep or worse, as I trudge through the snow to her truck. The wind whips my hair.

I look up at the stars. The night sky is so stuffed with them it looks as if it's sagging.

I open the back door.

"Please, Gah, let her survive."

TWO WEEKS LATER...

A thrill of hope, a weary world rejoices,
For yonder breaks a new and glorious morn.
Fall on your knees ——

Life is funny. Though of course when people say that, they mean just the opposite. Life is gruesome and bloody. From the moment you're born, the first way to check if you're alive is to make sure you can scream.

After hours in surgery, the ICU emergency team managed to put Libby's stomach back together and get her heart beating right. She woke up a few days later. Dom, Rosa, and I had been sitting in the waiting room in our various states of disarray—me in my sling, Dom in his wheelchair. We celebrated Christmas by napping on one another. At one point, Mildred came by with a gingerbread house and apologized for leading me to believe she was trying to abduct me—she just didn't want me to see the human head lolling on the ground at Frostbite. Then the doctors came in and announced the good news to Libby's parents that Libby was finally awake, and all of us went barging down the brightly lit hall, such a motley crew.

We ran into the Frieds at the ICU a few days later. They were draped in weird wooden beads and matching motivational T-shirts—the phrase *LIFE IS FUNNY* stamped across both their chests, which I guess is how the saying got lodged inside my brain. We hugged and talked about Davey. About the good news.

For Davey, good news means that while Dom and Rosa and I were squirming in Dr. Ferguson's basement, he opened his eyes for five minutes, then for ten minutes a few days later. Then a few hours after that, he looked around the room, and according to the nurse on duty, he said my name. (She is a self-described romantic, so I gave her the letters I've been writing him, and she promised she'd pass them along.) Good news also means that it was true that his blood-alcohol level was zero the night he was attacked. Before coming over to my house that night for dinner, Dr. Ferguson snuck through the Frieds' back door, jumped Davey, and injected him with enough liquid aspirin to make a horse keel over. Then he scattered the empty beer cans, came over to our place, and sat with us like nothing happened, like a maniac. Libby might have been lying, but in a way she was right. Whether or not Davey relapsed, he still ingested the aspirin, doctors thought. Only it was injected, not eaten—that's why the stomach pump didn't work. It was already in his bloodstream by then. He almost died.

I get to see him one night when the Frieds finally go home to sleep, during what they're saying is the biggest blizzard of the year.

At Libby's urging, I bribe the nurse who smuggled through my letters. One hundred bucks and a gas station gift card buys me three uninterrupted hours with someone I thought I'd never see again. I can't even count how many times I've wished for that kind of borrowed time with some of the people who have died on me. Mom, Ruth—even Ralph's parents, actually. But the best part about this is it's not a fantasy. And Davey is alive.

When he sees me duck through the door the look on his face is like I'm the one who almost disappeared, not him. The lights are off because he's supposed to be sleeping, but the moon is so bright in the window that I can see the stubble on his face. The snow is coming down in torrents of white fluff.

Instead of saying anything, he pulls back the covers and pats the thin strip of mattress beside him. We have never gotten to lie down together. We've never been alone like this.

I unstrap my walking cast, peel off my one sneaker, and limp toward him. We're grinning at each other—full smiles, teeth knocking teeth. His face is so scratchy that mine will be red for weeks.

They say he's going to have to do lots of physical therapy. But he can hug, and he can kiss, and he can rub his feet against mine, and trace a finger down the scar on my leg. And I'll tell you right now that when I touch him it's like every atom in his body is alive and buzzing and agile—I can feel it working.

So we both might be a little broken. But we fit together fine.

I would have happily stopped right there: content that most of us had survived, and comfortable in the knowledge that I'd testify in court in about a year—and that as a result, Ralph and Dr. Ferguson would suffer for the rest of their lives. Cloudy Meadows is facing an official investigation, and so is Green Bay Correctional Facility—for failing to update background checks on their mental health contractors (they didn't even know that Dr. Ferguson had been fired) and not having a clue about what one of their inmates was up to.

It turns out that Dr. Ferguson had gotten used to a pretty lavish lifestyle while working at Cloudy Meadows, and after he was fired, the state-funded visits to Ralph and a few sessions per week with me weren't enough to keep him solvent. He was facing foreclosure on his house, repo on his car, and he had been getting hounded by a bunch of other creditors for at least a month when Ralph made his fatal offer.

Money makes people crazy. I can't go five seconds without being reminded that evil exists, and that I can't do anything about it. Albus's face is plastered all around Wisconsin—a picture of her grinning, mouth full of braces, with that red plastic whistle looped around her neck—the one she said she'd blow if she ever needed me. She's been missing for two weeks now. Statistically and given the weather, it doesn't look good. But Staake's not helping (surprise, surprise) and every time I bring up Albus, or try to talk about what happened that night to Dom or Rosa or Libby, they all get quiet like they don't remember. I don't see flashes of her anymore—no more glimpses of her that end up being foliage or whatever—and I'm not sure what that means.

"Is this my life?" I asked Davey. "Just running from trouble to trouble?"

He says my getting so obsessed like this is a gift. But I don't know. It feels more like a compulsion bordering on sickness. People say that I've been through a lot for my age. But I'm starting to think that part of me must *want* to grapple with evil, otherwise it wouldn't seek me out. And what does that say about my sanity? Maybe someday I'll give in and learn how to own it a little—fall on my knees in the presence of destiny, live out whatever metaphor Davey hears when "O Holy Night" comes on.

In the meantime I've got a bone to pick with Ralph. After taking the Chewbacca head from Dr. Ferguson's basement and selling it online, I have hundreds of thousands of dollars in my PayPal account, so it was no problem to dole out a thousand to each of Ralph's guards in exchange for getting me in to see him.

Per my request, the guards have Ralph strapped upright in a restraint dolly, facing me from the other side of the double-plated glass. The guys locked up on either side of him are staring at me all wild-eyed from their respective cells, licking the glass or hissing "Slut" at me through the communication vents.

Luckily I also stipulated when handing out my payoffs that Ralph be silenced. So in addition to being forced to look at me, he's gagged with this complicated-looking bite guard thing, which the prisoners have to wear if they're prone to gnawing on themselves. Between the two of us, I'm the only one who will be doing any talking.

"The social life here seems really vibrant," I say,

gesturing at the cackling, hissing men on either side of him.

Ralph shuts his eyes like he's trying to ignore me, and I'm pretty sure I see a tear roll down his cheek.

I force myself to smile. The truth is, I'm barely holding it together. A guy fifteen feet to my left is frantically licking the glass, and another to my right is handcuffed behind his back so he won't touch himself in front of me.

I plop down on the metal chair that's been set out and just sit there for a while, forgetting everything I wanted to say. I gaze down at the shopping bag full of Whatchamacallit bars that I brought. I wanted to be mean. I wanted to torture him—I planned to eat these suckers right where he could see me until my stomach hurt because they're his favorite candy bars. But I can't do it. That's how he and I are different, it turns out, which is its own sort of relief and bad news at the same time. It'd be easier, in a way, if I could just take it out on him and feel better. But apparently that isn't how I'm built.

I pick up the shopping bag and get up, unable to look at him anymore. Outside in the parking lot, the wind screeches in my ears—and even though it's cold and awful in its own way, I remember the bars inside, and the smell of metal, and rejoice in the frigid weather, my freedom. My plans this evening are pretty typical for me lately: I'm stopping by the sheriff's department again to see if they found Albus. (Staake thinks I'm crazy still, and in a way maybe he's right: there's not much difference between insanity and pure, unfettered hope.) Then it's back to the hospital. Libby's still stuck there, and I've been sleeping in the empty bed next to hers, even on school nights. I'm sort of afraid something might happen to her if I don't. And the truth is I don't love being alone, either.

I cross the prison parking lot to my van. In the distance, snow-covered flatlands extend into a densely wooded stretch of leafless trees. My hands are ham-colored claws, and my ears are ringing from the cold—at least I think that's what I hear.

I stop stock-still and listen, clenching my teeth so they won't chatter, holding my breath so that nothing interferes. It could be the screaming wind, like it usually is. But somewhere in that passable expanse, I think I can hear the tiny vibrato of a plastic whistle.

"Albus," I whisper.

I shake my head. It couldn't be.

But then I hear it again.

ACKNOWLEDGMENTS

Thanks to Erica Sussman, Chris Hernandez, James Frey, Rosemary Stimola, and everyone at Full Fathom Five and Harper Teen who made this book possible.

Thanks also to my beloved readers: Patti, Chris, Sarah McKetta, and my husband, Simon Rich, all of whom have heard the sentences in here spun two different ways who knows how many times. And a big shout-out to the Brooklyn café Ted and Honey, the kind of place that doesn't care if you buy a croissant and a cup of coffee and hang around all day, and where a girl can write a novel if she wants to.

But thanks especially to my dad, the original Dominic Bushman, who is loving and hilarious, and a much better cook than the dad in this series. When I was a kid, he pressed Pause over and over again during our long drives to school so that he could explain the complicated layers of Bruce Springsteen lyrics (blue-collar ambition interlaid with memories of love long ago extinguished) and fill in the blanks between songs on the *Les Misérables* soundtrack (so that eventually I understood where Javert was coming from, and even the depravity of the innkeepers made some sense to me). At home, he and I watched movies based on the comic books he'd read as a child—movies that he also paused, about every ten minutes, so that he could explain each character's intricate backstory. And although I shrieked in frustration during these long digressions, my dad's love of the weird and epic ultimately fostered in me a love for storytelling. I have written countless terrible novels that could never be published, but he has always printed them out so he could mark by hand the parts that he loved best.

Small town.
BIG MURDER.

See where Kippy's story began.

An Imprint of HarperCollinsPublishers